The Hanuman Heart

Scharada Dubey

Illustrated by
Kishor Girdhari

VISHWAKARMA
PUBLICATIONS VP®

The Hanuman Heart

First published by Rupa & Co.- September, 2005
This Edition by Vishwakarma Publications - April, 2016

© *Scharada Dubey*

ISBN 978-93-85665-04-2

Published by:
Vishwakarma Publications
283, Budhwar Peth, Near City Post, Pune- 411 002.
Phone No: (020) 24448989 / 20261157
Email: info@vpindia.co.in
Website: www.vpindia.co.in

Cover Design : **Abhishek Darekar**

Typeset and Layout : **Chaitali Nachnekar**

Printed at : **Repro Knowledgecast Limited,** Thane

Dedication

*To Hanuman, who keeps me sane by
reminding me of my monkey origins
and devotees of Hanuman in India and
across the world.*

Introduction

This book of stories was written out of my intense love and devotion for Hanuman. It is a celebration of the most lovable and inspiring qualities of our beloved monkey-God. I am grateful that Hanuman found me worthy enough to relate his tales. I hope the readers

of these stories, both children and adult, find as much joy in the narration, as I have found in writing it. If they feel happier, braver, and more loving as a result of reading these stories, my work as an author will have been immensely rewarded.

Hanuman's life is an inspiration because most of us go through moments of mischief and laughter, sadness and doubt, triumph and trouble, like he did. However, he possessed a great medicine to deal with each one of life's situations - his love for Rama. And we can draw courage and strength from his actions.

To write this book, I have studied many Hanuman stories, and have been helped tremendously by the wealth of anecdotes and tales related in the 'Shri Hanuman Ank', the special annual issue of the forty-ninth year of publication, of the Gita Press, Gorakhpur, publishers of 'Kalyan'. The blessings of my guru, Sri Neeb Karori Baba, who was recognised as an incarnation of Hanuman, have kept me going, even on days when I have felt most like a failed devotee.

The first edition of this book was brought out by Rupa and Co. in 2005. I had sketched Hanuman's character with my own imagination, and was helped enormously by Vidya Mani, then editor of the children's magazine Chatterbox, who suggested improvements . Any faults in the book are my own, but l hope none of these is so big as to disappoint or trouble my readers.

One of the best things about growing up in India, is that we are never too far away from our personal God. If we want to feel an abiding love for Hanuman, we can always find him somewhere around us, on a calendar, in a painting, or a sculpture, or even in song and dance. He lives around us in many ways, alongside the multitude of worshipped icons beloved to millions – Durga and Sai Baba, Guru Nanak and Ambedkar, Jesus and the edifice of Mecca. But most importantly, apart from all the visual reminders on the outside, Hanuman lives in our hearts, just as Rama forever lives in his!

May this book place Hanuman at the center of your happy and' rejoicing heart!

Scharada Dubey

Acknowledgements

This second coming of The Hanuman Heart owes everything to Vishwakarma Publications, led by Bharat Agarwal, and my friends and colleagues who work there with me as a joyful team - Vishal Soni and Stanley Gabriel, Uttam Patil, Shraddha Awati Joshi, Minakshi Patil, Niting Jaigude, Chaitali Nachnekar, Abhishek Darekar, Tarang Gharpure, Dinesh Durgade, Meghnad Deodhar, Mamta Sarode, Kamal Kakade, Bharat Sargar, Mahendra Mahadik, Ketan Sonaskar, Kumar Kore, Kailas Ghodke and Sunil Shinde.

My mother, Madhu Dubey, who engages in satsang with me every chance we get, savouring various scenarios from the Ramcharitmanas, or singing a bhajan or two, is the single most important reason for me to have retained my love for God through my adult life and all the turmoil it represents. I feel blessed that she is here to see this re-issue of The Hanuman Heart. My daughter Shivani Bail, and son Shishir Bail have accompanied me on many journeys to Hanuman and other deities, and know it is the pilgrims whom I love as much as the God beloved to them. I feel grateful for their love and support, always.

Thanks are also due to my many liberal and atheist friends for looking on my devotion to Hanuman with an indulgent eye and being able to distinguish it from the Hindutva and hyper nationalism that has so clouded matters of faith in our country in the past few decades.

And most of all, thanks to my animal companions Bhola and Kamli, for not letting me forget that the purest, most untainted hearts are often those from the animal kingdom, not from among homo sapiens.

I am indebted to all who pick up this book for love and money, and hope I do not disappoint my readers in my depiction of The Hanuman Heart.

Contents

The Golden Baby Who Played With The Sun

What kind of a baby would leap up into the sky to try and eat the sun? That great big golden ball in the sky spells fire and flames. As for touching it - ouch! But for one special baby, blessed with mighty powers, the sun looked like a tasty fruit! Let's find out who this baby was, and how he met the sun.

Ages and ages ago, one of the most beautiful apsaras in the court of Indra, the lord of heaven, was Punjikasthala. She once laughed in the presence of a rishi, or sage, who had been praying and doing tapasya for many years. This meant that he had learnt to be without food and water, not moving for years and thinking only about God.

All this made him very powerful indeed.

When he heard Punjikasthala laughing, the rishi was enraged, and thought she was laughing at him. He turned to her in anger and said, "You mischievous imp! You laugh and make fun of me because I am just skin and bones after my tapasya! I banish you from heaven. You shall have to live on earth, and that too, as a monkey!"

Poor Punjikasthala stood trembling before the rishi. "Indeed I did not laugh at you, respected sage," she said. Her eyes were full of tears, and her hands folded in prayer. "Please don't send me to earth, and make me live as a m-m-monkey!'" she pleaded. The rishi looked at her tearful face and his heart melted a little. He decided to punish her a little less. Perhaps she really wasn't so naughty after all.

"You shall truly be a most beautiful monkey!" he said. "And you shall also have the power of turning into a human when you wish. But you still have to honour my words, leave heaven and go to earth." Saying this, he turned to leave, and Punjikasthala knew she had to soon come down to earth from heaven.

Some time later, Punjikasthala was born on earth as the baby daughter of a great monkey chief called Kunjar, who decided to name her Anjana. Anjana was a pretty child, and as she grew up, her kind and sweet nature made all the monkeys around her very happy.

When it was time for her to get married, her father gave her away, to a famous monkey warrior named Kesari. It was a grand and lively monkey wedding.

Kesari and Anjana lived with many other monkeys in the forests on the mountain of Kanchangiri. There was plenty to eat, they had no enemies, sages lived in ashrams all around them, and they had a very happy and comfortable life together. But for many years they had no children, and this made Anjana sad and worried. She longed for a child whom she could hold, and feed, and bathe, and tell stories to.

She began to pray very hard, for God to give her the gift of a child. Meanwhile, unknown to Kesari and Anjana, all the gods in heaven had approached Shiva, who sat in Mount Kailash with his wife Parvati, and had asked him for help in saving the people who lived on earth.

"A lot of terrible things are happening on earth. You must help to save the lives of the good, the innocent and the brave," they said.

Shiva seemed as if he was still deep in meditation. He opened his eyes just a fraction, and said, "I am aware of the happenings on earth." His voice sounded like the slow rumble of thunder in the heavens. "But Vishnu shall shortly be taking a human form, and living on earth, He shall know how to deal with the evil, the cruel and the unjust!"

The gods were still agitated. They continued to plead, "We feel it would be good if you too could be a part of this, O Vishveshvara!" they said. They were calling Shiva by the name that describes him as the Lord of the Universe. Shiva spoke again. "So be it," he said. "A part of me shall join Vishnu against earth's evil forces, Parvati too, shall lend her 'shakti' to this form, and this will be of great help to Vishnu to complete his task."

Satisfied, the gods turned away, but they were left wondering. Who would be this assistant to Vishnu, this combination of Shiva and Shakti's strength?

Anjana continued to pray for a child. She was advised by a sage named Matang, who told her to pray on the Vrishabhachal hill before Lord Venkateshwara. The famous Tirumala-Tirupati temple is situated on this hill. Anjana prayed so hard that even the sages doing tapasya around her began to look on her with respect. She stopped eating food or drinking water, and twelve years passed as if it had been a moment.

One day, she felt the breeze blow in a great gust over her as she sat, and opened her eyes. Vayu, the God of Wind, stood smiling before her. "What is it you want after so much prayer?" asked Vayu.

"O God, please let me have a child" said Anjana. Her voice sounded hoarse and strange to her own ears, since she had not spoken in a long time.

"Most devoted Anjana! You deserve the best possible child!" said Vayu. "I am pleased to bless you and Kesari with a child who shall have my speed, my ability to leap long distances, and my strength. I shall guard over this child, and he shall ever be in my protection."

Vayu blessed Anjana with these words, then disappeared from sight. A happy Anjana returned home to reside once more at Kanchangiri with Kesari, close to the lake of Pampa, where the forests were green and the monkeys frolicked around them.

Some days later, the whole monkey community was very excited, because Anjana was going to have a baby. There was much chattering and delighted 'whoo-whoo' sounds among them, because they knew this child would be very, very, special.

On a Tuesday in the month of Chaitra (between March and April), on a full moon day, Anjana's baby was born. All nature, and the entire planet seemed to be smiling upon this much awaited and blessed infant.

Mountains stood taller, as if trying to look at the baby by standing on tip-toe. Brooks gurgled down mountain sides in sheer delight. Trees blossomed, sending out new shoots, and buds burst into bloom as beautiful flowers. A contented air reigned among all the animals - even the small dung beetle hummed as he rolled a ball of cow dung!

Happiness was visible everywhere, and no wonder, Anjana's child was here!

He was tiny, as babies should be, but his little fist clutched a powerful weapon - the Vajra. He already wore the sacred thread, and his head had a small, glittering crown on it, His ears had golden 'kundal' or earrings in them. But more than all his ornaments, it was he himself who was extremely beautiful. His fur was golden in colour, so that he looked as if he glowed in the light. His ears were like small rose petals.

He opened his tiny mouth in a yawn to reveal small, perfect teeth. These were later to become big, fearsome teeth, but now they looked like pearls. His eyes were large, and brown. He looked at his mother, and she felt thrilled. Of course, the baby would take time to talk, but already, as he looked at her, his eyes shone with a great intelligence, as if he understood everything.

He was Anjana's son, so they named him 'Anjaneya', but his beauty caused him to be instantly given another name too, 'Sundar', meaning beautiful. Later, as he performed many acts of great courage, he would earn many other names. Now, while all who surrounded him were still under the spell of his beauty, he cried for the first time. Anjana lifted him up to comfort him. In a moment, he was content again in her warm hug.

Anjana and Kesari's happiness knew no bounds.

Anjana was a most attentive and loving mother, but little Anjaneya was growing fast, so she had to go farther into the forest every day to collect fruits and special berries. One morning, Kesari was away, and Anjana too, had left her sleeping infant for a short while. When he awoke, and did not find her nearby, he began to throw about his arms and legs and cry to draw attention. When this did not work, he tumbled out of his cradle, and began to crawl on the forest floor on his dimpled, podgy knees.

He crawled to a clearing, from where he saw the sun shining above - an orange ball in the sky.

Anjaneya thought this ball looked most tasty, exactly like the ripe and delicious fruits his mother had told him about. He reached out his plump arms to touch the ball. But it seemed to be quite far away. He knelt on the forest floor and thought, perhaps I should jump towards it. One leap launched him into the sky. He was blessed with the powers of Vayu, after all!

Anjaneya was delighted. He looked down at the green forest below him and the open sky all around him. To be floating free like this felt great! Now he began reaching towards the sun again, and his body began moving towards it with great speed.

Vayu saw Anjaneya speeding like a meteor towards the sun. He became very worried about the little infant getting burned by the rays of the sun if he got too close to it. He began blowing cool and icy breezes to protect the baby's skin from getting blistered.

The sun himself, whom the gods call Surya, was surprised to see Anjaneya come rushing towards him. He did not want to burn this most unusual infant either, So he dimmed his brightness, and turned pale and watery, so that Anjaneya would not be hurt.

Helped by the cooling winds of Vayu, Anjaneya arrived to where Surya was riding in the heavens on his chariot, driven by Arun. When he finally saw the sun, like a typical child, he forgot his original hunger for the 'sun fruit'. Instead, he began playing with Surya, who lifted him up and threw him up into the air while Anjaneya gurgled. After some time, he wanted to sit up in front of the chariot with Arun. He wanted to hold the reins of the vehicle that never stops moving in the sky.

Rahu, the dragon planet, arrived in the middle of this jolly scene. Rahu is permitted to make a meal of the sun and swallow him on Amavasya or new moon days. This happened to be one such day.

Rahu approached the playful threesome, snorting fiercely, and preparing to swallow the sun. Little Anjaneya did not like the way this stranger was coming towards his new friend. He swung his small fist and landed a nice blow on Rahu's face!

'A-a-a-h!' Rahu yelled, reeling at this mighty blow from a tot!

As if to repeat his feat, Anjaneya now got off the speeding chariot of the sun and began toddling towards the stricken Rahu. He had just raised his fist again when Rahu ran away, yelping. Surya chuckled and Anjaneya and he began playing again.

A sulking Rahu reached the court of Indra, the king of the gods.

'What injustice is this?' he asked Indra. 'You have awarded me the right to swallow the sun every month, but now it looks as if you have given this right to someone else too.'

'Have I?' asked a puzzled Indra. He was even more puzzled when Rahu related his whole tale of woe. He decided to climb on his heavenly white elephant,

Airavat, and go and see the scene for himself. Rahu, muttering angrily under his breath, accompanied him.

When they reached the sun, Anjaneya immediately recognized Rahu as his old enemy and gave chase. Rahu ran towards the sun, trying to swallow him. Airavat got startled at these sudden movements and harrumphed and raised his front legs. Anjaneya pulled his tail, picked him up in a single movement, and began swinging him around!

Indra was scared by the superhuman strength displayed by Anjaneya, a mere baby, and decided to use his most powerful weapon, the thunderbolt. He aimed this at Anjaneya, and it hit the baby on his chin, Instantly, baby Anjaneya fell down, unconscious, his chin broken by the impact of Indra's weapon.

The winds howled around this awful scene as Vayu realised what had happened to his beloved charge. He rushed and picked up the still form of Anjaneya, and went into a cave and shut himself up. He wept over the baby, sad that he had failed to protect Anjaneya when he had promised he would. When Vayu disappeared like this, the breeze stopped blowing in all the three worlds - earth, heaven and the lower kingdom of 'patal', where the demons lived. There was no air anywhere, and not a leaf, or a creature moved. Everything was suspended, like a film that has suddenly gone still.

Anjana and Kesari became still where they were. They had no idea of all that was happening up in the sky.

The gods rushed to Brahma, the creator of the worlds, and asked him to make Vayu blow the winds again. Brahma, accompanied by all the gods, entered the cave, where Vayu sat.

"Why are you here?' asked a distraught Vayu. 'Where were you when this little infant was being unjustly attacked by the strongest weapon Indra has?"

Brahma patted Vayu's back to soothe him. He then placed his hand on Anjaneya's forehead. The still, small infant began to move. In another moment, Anjaneya blinked, and sat up. All the assembled gods applauded. Vayu too, smiled in relief. The flow of air began to bring creatures everywhere to life once again.

Now Brahma blessed this special infant. "This child shall never be hurt by the 'Brahma shaap' (a terrible curse)," he said. "His body can never be destroyed by even the strongest weapons."

He turned to the gods and said, "Come forward and bless this extraordinary child. It is he who will protect you tomorrow from the evil might of demons and cruel people!"

Indra stepped forward and garlanded Anjaneya with a garland of heavenly lotuses. "My 'Vajra' (thunderbolt) has broken this poor child's hanu' (chin). Because of this, I am naming him Hanuman, and he shall be famous by this name. Never again will my thunderbolt work against him, and his body will be as hard and invincible as the 'vajra'"

Surya stepped forward and said, "He shall be brilliant like me, and I promise to complete his education and teach him all I know."

Varuna, the God of Water, stepped forward and said, "He need never fear any harm from water."

Kubera, the God of Wealth blessed Anjaneya with, "He shall never be defeated in battle. My 'gada' (the heavy mace) shall be his weapon, and he shall never be harmed by my armies of 'yakshas' and 'rakshasas'."

The blessings poured forth from all the gods, till a deep rumble announced the speech of Shiva. "So all of you have taken a liking for this infant! This is as it should be! He is that same assistant to Vishnu, that you had asked me to provide, with your prayers."

The gods were amazed to discover that this little child was to grow up and help save the earth from the cruel and the unjust. Now they looked with new eyes at the beautiful infant, He yawned, and fell asleep.

When he awoke, his mother was next to him, and he made a monkey sound of contentment. Soon he was settled in her lap.

So this is how Anjaneya got his powers. He was born gifted, but now he was blessed with gifts from all the gods, which gave him all their special qualities.

Little Anjaneya was already the mighty Hanuman!

A Curse &
An Education

Anjana and Kesari were worried parents.

After the gods had blessed him, they found it difficult to manage Hanuman's strength as well as his mischief. For Hanuman was far from being a meek and docile child. He liked nothing better than to romp around with all the animals in the forest. He lifted elephants up to test their weight, swung boars around by their curly tails, and raced other monkeys to the tops of tall trees. The poor animals found all this rough play sometimes quite difficult and tiring. But they kept silent, knowing Hanuman was good-hearted, not a bully.

Hanuman's mischief did not disturb only his animal companions. The forests around his mountain home held many ashrams where rishis prayed and did tapasya. Hanuman loved to make things turn lively around them, too. He would hang upside down from the thatched roof of an ashram where a rishi sat in meditation. The sage would open his eyes to find the upside down face of a monkey grinning at him, and this would startle him. He would take the seat of a rishi who had been practising sitting on a bed of nails. In its place, he would place the seat of another who had been sitting for some years on a piece of silk. Both rishis would jump up because their bottoms were used to sitting on something completely different!

Hanuman took holy water and played at doing 'puja'. He imitated the rishis' slow and solemn movements and irritated them. They were very tolerant most of the time. Those sages who had the ability to see the past, present, and future, knew that Hanuman would protect them one day. However, this did not make it much easier to bear some of his most naughty acts.

Kesari and Anjana worried about how they should get Hanuman to think about his actions. They wanted him to use his strength wisely, rather than scare others with its sheer force. But every time they thought they would talk to him about it, he looked so lovable that they could not scold him. He had innocent brown eyes, and his mouth turned up in a happy grin that made others smile in reply.

Anjana was a wise mother, and she knew this could not go on forever. She spoke to Kesari and suggested that they seek help from the sages who lived around them. Kesari agreed, and both of them approached a gathering of the rishis who had assembled for a yagna (prayer with holy fire).

"O sages," said Kesari, with folded hands, "God has blessed us with a most exceptional child. He has every power known to man and is most intelligent. There is not a single drop of ill-will in him. He is so good that we are unable to scold and criticise him. We don't know how to deal with him. His sheer playfulness gets him and others into trouble."

The sages nodded in agreement. They had all experienced Hanuman's 'playful' pranks.

"You have seen this child since he was born," said Anjana. "Please help us mould him into a fine adult. Let him be the pride of our family, this forest, and the whole world, with your blessings."

The rishis understood the plight of Hanuman's parents. They went into a huddle to discuss what they should do, After some time, three of the eldest rishis came forward to talk to Anjaneya's worried parents about what they had decided.

"We have decided that our best course of action will be a curse," they said.

"A c-curse!" both Anjana and Kesari were stunned.

"Do not worry, dear Kesari and Anjana. This curse is being given to protect your son," said the eldest sage. "And others too," murmured another elderly sage. It was he who had had to sit on silk when he should have been sitting on nails!

"Our curse is simply this. Hanuman shall forget he is strong, and not remember it till he is much older. Till then, he will be able to use his mighty powers only when someone reminds him by telling him that he is strong."

"Thank you, respected sages," said Anjana and Kesari. They bowed and left, but secretly they were wondering how this curse would help their son.

They need not have worried. While these awful words cursing Hanuman were being spoken by the rishis, he was already forgetting what it felt like to be the strongest person on earth. He was playing hide and seek with some other monkeys at that moment. They were crashing through the forest branches, but suddenly, he stopped and leapt to the ground. He took a deep breath. Everything felt different.

While before, he had looked at a distant mountain, and known he could reach it in a second, now it looked very far to him. Trees looked tall. The sky looked vast.

The animals, those creatures who had borne the brunt of his rough games, looked as if they could get hurt,

At that moment, a great change came over Hanuman.

He had been born with a strong, large, fearless heart. But now, something else came and filled his heart. A soft, kind emotion, that made him understand how the smallest and weakest of creatures must feel in a world much larger than themselves.

Hanuman's heart swelled. It grew and grew, and filled with compassion. Now he knew he had to always protect the meek, the small, the frightened and helpless. A great kindness settled over him, and it would always stay with him.

When he met Anjana and Kesari returning from their meeting with the sages, his mother was able to notice the change immediately. She greeted her son, hiding her private worry, and they made their way home together.

Hanuman began spending more time at home, listening to stories and teachings. He took great care not to hurt the forest animals or trees. He would still swing from trees and leap about but if he saw a thin branch ahead, he made himself lighter, so that the branch would not break under his weight!

He began to be a real friend of the small and humble animals, who looked up at him with stars in their eyes.

It was not only that his heart had grown - he was also growing bigger. When he was a baby, his mother had wrapped him in golden yellow cloth. Even his diaper was golden yellow. Now he wore a silk dhoti, which he wore down to his knees. To do justice to his monkey antics, he could not wear it to his ankles. The colour of his dhoti was always sunflower yellow, or hibiscus red, or a bright orange like the inside of a ripe mango.

His golden fur shone brightly, especially when it was touched by the rays of the sun. Below the fur, his body was tough and muscular.

He was becoming an adult with a body as hard as Indra's 'vajra', which would earn him the name of 'Vajrang' or 'Bajrang' as he is commonly called. His chest was broad and his shoulders were powerful. His tail was long, and had the strength of a hundred horses. But his most beautiful feature were his eyes. They shone with intelligence, and a kindness softened their brown gaze. Whoever saw him felt attracted to Hanuman.

This period in Hanuman's life was very important for his development. His mother, Anjana, had the power of seeing into the future. She was no ordinary monkey. She had been born on earth after living in heaven, and most of the stories she told Hanuman were about God. She told him how Vishnu appeared in various forms on earth - as a fish, or boar, or dwarf. She also described how he would return as Sri Ramachandra, the king of Ayodhya. Because of her heavenly powers, Anjana described the events of the Ramayana to her son, while he was still a child.

After some days it became evident that this story was the only one Hanuman wanted to hear, again and again. He listened intently to the part when Rama was helped by the great monkey Hanuman. At this, Hanuman would jump up in excitement. His fur would stand up all along his spine, his eyes would shine, his tail would swish and dance, and he would yell, 'That's me! I'll be that monkey! I'm going to help Rama!'

His mother would smile and quiet him down and pat his head.

"Of course you will my dearest You will help Rama cross every hurdle. Everyone who calls on you will be blessed by your strength and kindness!"

Sometimes she gave him a hug with these words and he became still. But sometimes he squirmed in her hug . Wriggling to get away, making a face as if he was being tricked, he wanted to continue thinking about the story It was obvious that Hanuman loved to imagine the story of Rama and his own future role in it This was what he dreamed of when he was a child.

As he listened to the story An]ana told, Hanuman would jump up and punch the air or swing his golden mace. These antics made his father happy. Kesari was glad to see his son display such courage and enthusiasm. He himself was a famous warrior.

His mother noticed how he loved to hear about Rama and said, "It is natural that you should feel this way about Rama, dear. You shall be his best friend. It is to serve him that you were born."

Thus Hanuman began to say aloud the name of his future friend.

He could not wait to meet him and begin their adventures together. He began spending long hours by himself in the forest saying "Rama Rama Rama". He would wander over mountains and valleys or cross rivers and sit for hours on a rugged peak Often his mother or father would have to go in search of him and bring him back home to feed him. After hours spent saying the name of God, Hanuman was not hungry. Still, his mother would lovingly put some morsels in his mouth and he would eat, only to repeat the scene the next day.

When Hanuman grew a little older, his parents wanted to complete his education. They remembered

Surya, the sun god's promise to teach him. They called Hanuman to their side, and said, "You need to spend time with a guru to master what you will need to know in your adult life. So we are sending you to Surya the sun god. There is nothing he does not know, and he has promised to teach you himself."

Anjaneya agreed, but spoke aloud to say, "How far away the sun is! How will I reach there? Are you taking me?" It was then his parents understood the working of the sages' curse. They smiled and reminded him, "The distance is nothing to you. You can leap any distance, and have the power to fly with great speed, like Vayu, the god of wind."

Now Hanuman remembered his power, and took leave of them.

He streaked like a meteor across the sky again, and reached the setting sun. "O Surya, my parents send you their greetings, and request that you should accept me as a pupil and teach me what I need to know," he said.

Surya the sun god smiled and said, "Having a student like you will be an honour indeed!" He remembered this radiant monkey as a playful baby.

"But there is only one difficulty," Surya continued. "Do you see this chariot? I can never leave it, and neither can Arun, the charioteer, ever stop it. I have to keep racing across the heavens, or three worlds will come to a standstill. If I cannot keep still, how will I teach you?"

"I do not have to stand still to learn, and you need not stand still to teach," replied Hanuman. "I will just keep running in front of your chariot, and you must keep saying what you want me to remember. We will soon be done."

Surya was even more pleased. He knew that Hanuman was really a form of Shiva, protected by Vayu, blessed with the fine qualities of all the gods. He knew that Hanuman did not really need to submit himself to a teacher, since he was born to help God, However, by becoming a student, Hanuman was showing the way to people on earth, who must obey the simple rule of submitting to a teacher in order to learn.

Hanuman was learning from Surya, so that for ever after, the guru-shishya or student-teacher relationship would be respected.

He raced around the heavens while Surya taught him the Vedas, all forms of knowledge, and wisdom necessary for him as an adult.

Hanuman was preparing for his life adventures.

Mangal moorat, maarut nandan,
sakal amangal mool nikandan,

Pavan tanay santan hitkaari,
hriday biraajat ajar behari.

The most auspicious form,
son of Maarut, who uproots all forms of evil,

Born of the wind, helpful to all saints,
in whose heart dwells deathless Sri Rama.

How Hanuman
Met Rama

Hanuman completed his studies and prepared to part from Surya, the Sun God who had been his teacher. Surya said, "I am confident that your knowledge shall always be used to protect the good, the humble and all those who need your help. When you reach back home, remember to keep an eye on my son Sugreev, who lives in the kingdom of Kishkindha. I shall be grateful for any manner in which you can assist him."

This request from his teacher held great importance for Hanuman. He promised to be of help to Sugreev. Then he streaked across the heavens to return home again to his loving parents, Kesari and Anjana.

His parents were delighted to have him back. But they began worrying again quite soon, They noticed that their son was developing a quiet and meditative nature. He liked best to be alone, with only God's name as his constant companion. If he was like this as a youth, how would he complete all his adult duties? Kesari was a warrior, a general in the army of King Hriksharaja who had ruled over the kingdom of Kishkindha. He wanted Hanuman to grow up to protect the kingdom too. Anjana too, wanted her son to become a brave and respected warrior.

Hanuman's parents decided to send him from Kanchangiri to Pampapur, the capital of Kishkindha. This was a beautiful kingdom of rocky mountains, green valleys and forests. Sparkling rivers and brooks flowed here. Trees laden with fruits fed the citizens of the kingdom - thousands and thousands of monkeys!

By the time Hanuman arrived in Pampapur, King Hriksharaja had passed away. The kingdom was ruled by his elder son Vali, a formidably powerful monkey. Vali was so fierce that he was able to keep away all the enemies and demons in the surrounding kingdoms. Vali shared a very loving relationship with his younger brother Sugreev. This was the same Sugreev whom Surya had asked Hanuman to protect.

When Hanuman arrived in Kishkindha both Vali and Sugreev greeted him most warmly. He had to learn about the kingdom and how it was run, and Vali wanted to teach him this. But remembering his promise to Surya, Hanuman spent more time with Sugreev, and the two became firm friends.

At this time, a cruel twist of fate caused the two brothers to become enemies forever.

One dark night, a great roaring was heard at the gates of Kishkindha. It was the demon Mayavi, who stood and challenged Vali to a fight. He shouted to Vali to come out if he dared.

Vali awoke from deep sleep and immediately rose to answer the demonic challenge. He went into the forest chasing the fearsome demon, and Sugreev went along too.

The demon seemed to have disappeared in the dark forest. Then they came upon a huge pit covered with leaves and grasses that led down deep into the ground. Vali entered this pit in pursuit of the demon, and asked his brother to stand guard at the mouth of the pit. He asked Sugreev to be there for a mere fifteen days, but Sugreev waited a whole month without his brother returning. He grew very worried.

His worst fears seemed to be coming true, for whenever he put his ear to the mouth of the pit and heard the underground roar of hundreds of demons. When he saw a thin stream of blood emerge from the pit one day, he could bear no more. He dragged a huge boulder to cover the mouth of the pit, and returned to

Kishkindha. He was sure his brother had died fighting the demon, and he mourned for him.

When Sugreev returned alone, the monkey ministers were very sad to hear about the loss of their brave king. Since Vali's son Angad was still a child, they appointed Sugreev as king in Vali's place, and he began to rule Kishkindha.

Meanwhile Vali emerged out of the pit as a proud victor who had fought and killed hundreds of demons single-handed. He reached Kishkindha to find his brother on the throne. He suspected Sugreev of treachery, thinking that he had deliberately blocked the entrance to the pit in order to snatch the kingdom. Angry Vali attacked Sugreev and snatched from him his wife Ruma. Sugreev had to run in terror to save his life. Hanuman accompanied him as he fled, Vali had sworn to destroy his younger brother, and Hanuman knew it was his duty to protect him.

Poor Sugreev had to search hard to find a place where he would be safe from Vali. But Hanuman had a keen and all-knowing memory.

Hanuman remembered a place where Vali was forbidden to enter - Sage Matang's ashram on the mountain of Hrishyamuk. He asked his friend to hurry and ask the sage to shelter him.

Vali could never enter Sage Matang's ashrarn because of an earlier incident. Some years before this, he had fought a demon named Dundubhi. Dundubhi was a bull, and threatened Vali's life and kingdom. Vali picked up the demon by the horns, swung him around, and threw him up in the sky. Dundubhi was killed when he landed on the ground. Unfortunately, a few drops of his demon blood splashed on to Sage Matang, who was walking in his forest ashram. The Sage was furious, and deeply upset by the sight of the blood. He was moved to pronounce a curse. "Whoever has caused this to happen to me, shall never be able to set foot in my ashram!" he declared. "If he ever tries to enter this space, his head shall blow itself into a thousand pieces!"

The awful words of the curse reached the ears of Vali, and he knew he must take care never to step into the ashram of Sage Matang.

Now Sugreev and Hanuman reached this haven and Sage Matang agreed to give them shelter, They began living here with a few of Sugreev's most devoted monkeys. Vali ruled in Kishkindha with his wife Tara, as well as Sugreev's wife Ruma as his queens. He continued to plot revenge on his brother. Sugreev was always afraid that one of his agents or soldiers would catch him and take him to Vali. He relied on Hanuman to be ever vigilant and alert.

One day, from the top of Hrishyamuk mountain, Sugreev and his friends spotted two tall and handsome youths making their way through the forest. These men wore simple clothes and had knotted their hair like forest-dwellers. But they carried the large and heavy bows that princes usually had as weapons. Seeing them, Sugreev was afraid that they may have been sent by Vali to first win him over, then kill him. He asked Hanuman to leave at once, meet the two visitors before they could reach Sugreev, and find out what was in their minds.

"If they seem to be enemies in disguise, signal to me and I shall leave immediately for some other place," said Sugreev. "If they are friends, bring them here, so we may receive them."

The two visitors were none other than the Ayodhya princes, Rama and Lakshman. They had been sent into exile by their father, King Dasharath. Both had spent thirteen years in the Chitrakoot and Dandakaranya forests, along with Rama's wife, Sita. In the fourteenth and last year of their exile, they were living in a leaf cottage at Panchavati, when a demon named Marich had appeared as a golden deer, to attract Sita's attention.

When she asked Rama to fetch her this unique deer, he went in search of it into the forest. A short while later, Marich began calling for help, imitating the voice of Rama and making it seem as if Lakshman must rush to rescue him. Sita urged and ordered her brother-in-law to go and see what had happened to Rama. When both Rama and Lakshman were absent, Ravana, the king of Lanka, abducted Sita.

Now the brothers were in search of Sita, and had come south in this search, as far as the kingdom of Kishkindha.

Hanuman felt a great excitement when Sugreev asked him to meet the visitors. He was sure that something wonderful, a miraculous event, was about to occur. But what was it to be? Not since he first heard the stories of Rama's adventures from his mother had he felt this excited.

He went leaping through the forest towards the strangers, taking care to wear the disguise of an old Brahmin. His true identity was to remain concealed, in case these were indeed Vali's agents.

Hanuman reached the two young men. He stood, an old Brahmin with folded hands in their path. As they approached him, he observed them keenly. The taller and older of the two youths was dark, while the other was fair-skinned. Both had the well-formed features that spoke of royal blood, In addition, they carried the heavy, princely bows.

But their clothes were worn, even torn. And their feet were protected from the rough jungle ground by wooden sandals.

When they stood before him, Hanuman bowed and spoke with extreme politeness, "Most respected guests! Everything about you shows that you are from a noble and distinguished family. Then why do you walk about in this desolate jungle, without a single servant? Your faces shine like the faces of gods. Are you the human forms of Brahma, or Vishnu, or Mahesh? Or such humans who can inspire thousands with their goodness? There are thorns, and stones and pebbles on this forest soil. Must they not be hurting your feet? Please tell me who you are, so I may have the opportunity to serve you in whatever way I can."

His polite words and respectful manner had their effect on the two strangers. They stopped, and the dark one said to his companion, "This is no ordinary person standing before us. The way he speaks shows he is most learned. Let him know who we are."

The fair stranger turned to Hanuman, bowed slightly, and said, "'You have noticed correctly that we are princes. This is my elder brother Rama, and I am Lakshman. We were sent into exile by our father, King Dasharath of Ayodhya, and while we were at Panchavati, Rama's wife was abducted by a demon. It is in Search of her that we have come this far south."

Hanuman heard Lakshman's speech with his ears, but his eyes were fixed on Rama. He was drinking in the sight of his most beloved Rama as if he could never again take his gaze away. This was the moment he had been dreaming of since he was a child!

He looked up into Rama's big and beautiful eyes, which were full of kindness and love, and his own filled with tears of joy. He fell at Rama's feet, then spoke in a voice full of agony, "O my Lord, is it really you? Forgive me for not having recognised you. I am not wise or learned at all, just a foolish, dim-witted monkey! Please say you forgive me."

With this, he fell again before Rama.

Rama continued to look at Hanuman. But he stayed silent. This was because Hanuman still wore his disguise, and God dislikes deception. Rama was God himself come down to earth. When standing before God, a devotee must be absolutely truthful, honest and unafraid.

Rama was waiting for Hanuman to show his true form. But Hanuman had forgotten he was in disguise! He was miserable that his beloved Rama still did not speak to him. He said, "I failed to recognise my Master because I am a mere monkey. But what about you Lord? How can you fail to recognise me, when I have been born only to serve and love you? How can you not know me, your own Hanuman?" In his despair, Hanuman tore at his hair, and the old Brahmin's wig came off! Now he remembered he was still in disguise, and threw off the rest of it.

Rama stepped forward and said, "Beloved Hanuman, I was just waiting for you to reveal yourself." Saying this, he folded Hanuman in a powerful hug, and at last Hanuman's thirst to be known by Rama was satisfied. It made a strange and wondrous sight. All the forest animals stopped what they were doing to take a look. Their mighty monkey friend was huddled small and tight in Rama's embrace. He was crying like a baby at what he had been through, when he thought Rama had not recognised him.

Hanuman's meeting with Rama was a crowning moment in his life.

When he could speak again, Hanuman told Rama and Lakshman the story of Sugreev, and what he had suffered at the hands of Vali.

"He is living the life of an exile in the forest, just like you," he told Rama. "And he is separated from his wife Ruma, like you have been separated from Sita. If you could become his friend and protect him at this time, he could be of great use to you." When he heard this, Rama agreed to befriend Sugreev.

Now Hanuman placed Rama on one powerful shoulder, and Lakshman on another. Then, in this joyous manner, he began carrying them to Sugreev. When Sugreev saw this from the mountaintop, he understood that these visitors were exceptional friends. A warm welcome awaited Rama and Lakshman when they arrived where Sugreev was staying.

That night, before a holy fire, Rama and Sugreev promised to do whatever was in their power, to help each other. Hanuman, who had brought about this friendship, sat content by their side.

In the firelight, his gaze remained fixed on Rama. At last, he was in a position to be of service to his Lord.

The Leap to Lanka

Sugreev's friendship with Rama made him offer thousands of bears and monkeys to the task of searching for Sita. Sugreev had become king of the monkeys again, after Vali was killed by Rama. He called the vast army of animals to assemble before Rama, and instructed them to go out in all the four directions and bring word of Sita.

"Set out now, and bring news of Mother Sita back to Rama, within a month. Remember, all of you! If you come back after a month from this day, to show your miserable faces, you will have to face a terrible death - I shall kill you myself!" said Sugreev, fiercely. He wanted to make sure that all the monkey and bear warriors should have a clear idea of how urgent their task was.

Indeed the task was urgent, and a difficult one too. Rama's eyes were full of the pain of separation from his beloved wife. He often looked sadly into the distance.

Although he would smile at the antics of his monkey friends, and respond most lovingly to their attention, it was obvious that he was missing Sita terribly. Hanuman was yearning to make him happy again.

He was eager to begin the search for Sita, no matter how far it led.

All the monkeys formed themselves into groups with their bear companions, and began leaving for different destinations after bowing to Sugreev and Rama. Hanuman was headed south, with Vali's son Prince Angad, the old and wise bear Jambavant, and monkey warriors Nala, Sushen, Sharabh, Maind and Dwivid. A large band of ordinary monkey and bear soldiers accompanied them.

When it was time to leave, Rama called Hanuman aside. "Of all the friends around me, I know that you are the one most eager to complete this difficult task," he said. "Since I met you in the forest, I have seen your strength, your wisdom, your humility and courage. I am extremely grateful for your great love for me, and feel most confident that you shall be the one to find Sita."

Hanuman felt very moved by these words. He was bending to fall at Rama's feet, but Rama held him by the shoulders. He looked deep into Hanuman's eyes and said, "Sita will not know you, never having seen you before. You must earn her trust, so that she knows you have come from me. Take my ring to give to her." He slipped his royal ring from a finger of his right hand, and gave it to Hanuman. "When you see her, tell her how much I miss her and how I can hardly wait to free her from the clutches of the demon who took her away!" Rama's eyes were filled with pain, but his jaw was firm with determination. Hanuman was determined to do the best for Rama, yet torn by grief at having to go away from him. He touched Rama's feet, and said, "I shall do exactly as you say."

The journey south was long and difficult. At one point, the group of brave monkeys and bears was wandering hungry and parched with thirst, through a thorny, dry, scrub jungle, Here, they were helped by a yogini named Swayamprabha, who presided over a beautiful garden of fruit trees and fresh water brooks. This was reached by entering a dark cave. Hanuman discovered the entrance to this cave, and the group was able to move on, refreshed.

Some days later, they reached land's end. The band of monkeys and bears stood helplessly on a sandy shore, while a vast ocean stretched before them. A strong sun beat down upon their bare heads.

"It is close to thirty days since we set out," said Nala. "How are we going to cross this huge ocean?"

"Uncle Sugreev said he will finish us if we fail in our mission," said Angad. He lay down, exhausted, on the sand. "It looks as if we have to call it quits here. I think I will die here rather than return to die in disgrace.

Sharabh looked up and said, "There is already an old vulture circling above our heads to see if he can make a tasty meal." And sure enough, there was an old vulture flying towards them.

But luckily for Sugreev's search party, this vulture was Sampaati, brother of the great bird Jatayu. When Ravana had been carrying Sita away, Jatayu had attempted to stop him. He had been badly injured fighting Ravana, it was because of Jatayu that Rama had discovered exactly how Ravana had escaped with Sita. Jatayu had spent the last moments of his life cradled in Rama's arms.

Now Sampaati spoke to Hanuman and his companions. From him, they found out that Ravana had taken Sita to his kingdom Lanka, which lay across the sea. "If I had not been old and feeble, I might have tried to stop the demon king" said Sampaati. "It was a sad sight indeed to see Ma Sita crying and calling out to be saved from that 'rakshasa'. Her hair was loose and she was shedding pieces of her jewellery as he flew away with her."

Hanuman and his group were shocked at this mental picture. "If you want to take news of Ma Sita back to her husband, you will have to cross the ocean and enter Lanka," concluded Sampaati, "Ravana keeps her prisoner in a heavily guarded place."

These simple words threw the group from Kishkindha into confusion. "Who will cross the ocean?" the cry went up.

"I can jump ten 'yojanas'," said a soldier named Gaja. (Yojana was an ancient unit to measure distance). "I can jump twenty," said another soldier, Gavaksh. Then each person present came forward with his own ability. "I could jump a hundred yojanas at one time, but do not think I can jump the whole distance. And anyway, I doubt whether I can return after fighting the fearsome soldiers and rakshasas guarding Ravana's palace," said Angad, finally.

All this while, Hanuman was sitting quietly, looking across the ocean, with his mind full of sad thoughts. Why was he unable to help Rama? Why was he so unworthy of the trust that Rama had placed in him? When he thought of how Rama had spoken to him when he was leaving, saying, "You shall be the one to find Sita.." he felt absolutely terrible.

This was the effect of the childhood curse of the rishis on Hanuman. Blessed with the strength and qualities of every single god, he was unable to remember his own strength!

Besides, his love for Rama was so great, that he could barely spare a thought for himself.

When he sat on the shore, he was only remembering Rama's agony, Rama's separation from Sita, Rama's trust in him... He could hardly even remember his own name at that moment!

Jambavant came ambling up to Hanuman, and sat down beside him. "And what are you thinking about, most brave and gifted Anjaneya?" he asked. "Are you thinking about how you can leap across to Lanka? Or what you are going to do to the rakshasas who challenge you? You have tried to swallow the sun in your childhood! Can you ever fail to carry out the toughest tasks in the universe?"

Jambavant patted his young friend's shoulder. "You were born to serve Sri Rama with all the power and courage that you possess. Why hesitate now?" The old bear could see that Hanuman looked dejected. He was doing his best to remind Hanuman of his own strength.

And what a transformation he brought about!

Under the spell of his voice, and encouraged by]
ambavant's hand on his shoulder,

Hanuman's whole body seemed to expand! A surge of
superhuman strength ran through him. He stood up,
and looked tall and magnificent, with his broad chest
and golden hair glinting in the light of the sun. He
looked at the ocean, and it suddenly seemed a most
simple task for him to leap across its blue depths.

Hanuman opened his mouth wide to reveal big,
fearsome teeth and roared with sheer abandon! The
huge sound echoed back from all four sides, and the
ground vibrated with its force. All the soldiers from
Kishkindha huddled together for a few seconds in
fright. Then they realised it was their friend's battle
cry, and set up a loud cheer.

Hanuman turned to Jambavant. "Thank you for
reminding me what I can do. Shall I destroy every last
rakshasa in Lanka, and bring back Sita?" Hanuman's
eyes were large and brown, and extremely fierce. It
looked as if no power in the universe could now stand
in his way.

Jambavant smiled and said, "Destroying Ravana and
punishing him for what he has done is Rama's right.
He shall bring Sita home. Your job is only to complete
the task set for you by Rama. Take news of Sita back
home to him, and let him do the rest."

Hanuman took a deep breath. "You are indeed kind to remind me of my duty as well as my strength. he said. "And now, with your blessings, I shall be on my way." So saying, he leapt up to the top of a nearby mountain named Mahendra Parvat.

When Hanuman landed on the mountain, huge chunks of it began to break away from the peak and scatter in the surrounding area. For a few minutes, the band of monkeys and bears looked up in awe to see the mighty figure of their friend outlined against the sky. Hanuman closed his eyes and thought of his parents, Anjana and Kesari, Vayu the Wind God who ever protected him, and his guru Surya. Then, with all his heart and mind he remembered Rama, and his parting words to himself.

Finally, he spoke to his friends. "Do not worry. I feel completely capable of jumping to Lanka and returning with news of Ma Sita. Not only has God been kind enough to give me great strength, he has blessed me by appearing as my Lord Rama, and trusting me with this task! Knowing this is enough to give me the courage to leap over a thousand oceans! Please wait for me at this place, till I return. I shall try to come back as soon as I possibly can."

As he spoke these words Hanuman appeared so brilliant that it seemed as if he was aflame, and sparks were emanating from him.

There was no trace of the poor-spirited sadness that he had shown a short while before. His friends had no hesitation in imagining that his leap to Lanka would be a success. Ramdoot – the messenger of Rama – would never disappoint his Lord.

Turning towards Lanka, Hanuman raised his right hand skyward. Then Rama's name came to his lips, and he lifted off the ground with great speed. What were the tests and trials he would have to face before reaching Lanka?

Hanuman flew towards Lanka feeling wonderful to be flying again. He felt grateful for the breeze that blew against him, and for the speed and strength that he had found anew.

Below him, a large island raised itself out of the waters of the ocean, as if inviting Hanuman to take rest on its forested slopes, It was the mountain Mainaak, commanded by the gods to provide the first test for Hanuman in his mission.

"Relax and take a few deep breaths on my shoulder, O Pavankumar!" said Mainaak, calling Hanuman by one of the names given to him by the gods, He raised his peak even higher, as if to touch Hanuman as he passed. But Hanuman was very conscious of the importance of his task. He was not going to waste valuable time in resting on an island, however inviting it looked.

"Many thanks, dear friend, for your kind offer," said Hanuman. "I will take advantage of your hospitality some other time. Now I have to reach Lanka with all possible speed." Hanuman hurried ahead, touching the tip of the mountain affectionately as he passed. Mainaak retreated, satisfied that Ramdoot had passed his first test while doing his duty.

The next test was much more demanding. A giant, monstrous sea creature with huge, open jaws and flaming yellow eyes the size of small islands, lay in wait for him in the water. This was Surasa, a she-demon who had been sent to test Hanuman's determination and cleverness, while performing his task.

"O brave Hanuman," she called, "The gods have sent you here today to be a tasty meal for me. I am extremely hungry. Come and satisfy my hunger by letting me swallow you!"

From high above her, Hanuman folded his hands and said, "O mighty Surasa Ma! I am going with all speed to complete Rama's job. I cannot delay even a moment, nor can I die before I have done what I should! Please forgive me. When I have met Ma Sita, and gone back to give this news to Rama, I shall return and enter your mouth myself. Today, I just have to go."

Surasa was secretly pleased, but she outwardly insisted, "Try and escape me if you can - you are just the meal I needl" Saying this, she opened her jaws sixteen yojanas wide, and the ocean turned black with the sight of her immense mouth. But Hanuman was equal to this.

He increased his own size to a huge, thirty two yojana wide giant monkey. How could such a large creature fit into Surasa's jaws? Every time Surasa opened her jaws wider, Hanuman grew larger! Finally she opened her mouth to cover a distance of a hundred yojanas, and Hanuman made himself the size of a small fly or gnat. Quickly, he flew into her mouth, and before she could close it, he had flown out again.

Now he resumed his normal shape and flew up and said, "I have already entered your mouth, and satisfied the gods, if they wanted me to be a morsel for you. Now, dear Surasa Ma, please let me go and complete my task!"

Pleased with his intelligence and his devotion to Rama, Surasa said, "O Hanuman! It was my fortune to have been able to meet you in your mission. Go and complete your task with all my blessings!"

Thus blessed, Hanuman continued towards Lanka. He could now see it as a green and scenic island in front of him. He did not want to approach it in the daytime, and waited till night had fallen. Then he approached the heavily guarded gates of Lanka, deciding to adopt his small insect form, so that he could escape detection.

But Lankini, the guardian goddess of Lanka, spotted him and called out, "Who is this, trying to enter the city, in this tiny form? Show yourself, if you value your life!"

Hanuman hesitated. He did not want to have a big fight with Lankini because the noise this would make would alert all the other rakshasas guarding Lanka. He also did not want to hit her very hard, because she was a woman. But answering her challenge was necessary.

If he did not, she would raise an alarm, and alert others. Hanuman would not be able to search for Sita. So he resumed his normal shape, and gave a soft, left-handed hit to Lankini's jaw.

Lankini reeled under this mild hit. For some moments, she saw only stars, and heard bells ring in her ears. When she recovered and sat up, she looked up with awe at Hanuman. "So you are the monkey that the gods had told me about! You are the messenger of Rama whose wife Ravana has captured! I was told that Lanka's demons would meet their end soon after you had crossed this gate, and laid me low with a single blow! Well, what was predicted has happened, and I can only now wish you well. Go forward, brave messenger! Do what you have to do."

What more did Ramdoot need to move ahead with his task? He bowed to Lankini, and entered the golden kingdom of Lanka.

At Sita's Feet

In the darkest hour of night, Hanuman moved around the well-guarded city of Lanka looking for Sita. He saw tall majestic buildings decorated with carved doors. He saw demon sentries at each street corner holding aloft great flaming torches. He had to move around in his small insect like form in order not to be discovered.

Hanuman approached the huge gold painted buildings where Ravana lived. This palace had many gates all guarded by burly sentries holding fearsome weapons. It had many terraces and balconies with a view of the city and the sea. It glowed golden in the darkness.

Hanuman entered the palace by a side door and soon came upon a courtyard where a chariot covered with flowers was parked. This was the Pushpak Vimana or flying chariot Ravana used it to fly to distant destinations.

Hanuman spent some moments examining it then hurried inside.

He lightly ran up the stairs to a hall where guards and courtiers had fallen asleep around a grand throne. There were plenty of empty wine glasses, and the leftovers of a lavish dinner. Hanuman did not see any sign of Sita, so he quickly left this hall, and moved towards Ravana's sleeping quarters.

The demon king was snoring on a huge, decorated bed. Some maidens, holding fans in their slim fingers, had fallen asleep in their task of fanning the king. Others had curled up next to the instruments they had been playing for the king's amusement.

Hanuman had never seen so many women, and he quickly scanned their faces before concluding that none of them was Sita.

In the next room, another richly decorated bed was placed in the center. When Hanuman peeped at the female figure asleep there, he was struck by her beauty. Instantly imagining that such beauty could only be Sita's, he felt happy to have found her. He began to do a monkey dance of merriment all around the room, silently prancing and swishing his tail.

However, in another moment, he had sobered up. He was thinking, "This most beautiful lady is covered with expensive jewellery, and dressed in silks. Sampaati the vulture had described Ma Sita dropping her jewels as she cried Sri Rama's name. Besides, this lady sleeps a peaceful and unworried sleep. Can Ma sleep like this when she is separated from her beloved husband? I am sure I have made a mistake in thinking this is Ma. Most likely it is someone else."

Hanuman was absolutely right in thinking thus. The sleeping lady was Ravana's queen Mandodari, Hanuman hurried through the remaining rooms of the palace, and not finding Sita, began a tour of the city.

He saw demon families asleep in some homes. In some others, demons gambled and drank, sometimes fighting among themselves.

He saw mothers cuddling their children, and heard the coughs and groans of elderly demons. But of Sita, there was no sign. Hanuman paused in his task, tired and slightly discouraged. Dawn was approaching, and it was the auspicious hour before sunrise.

Imagine Hanuman's surprise and delight, when, in this quiet hour, he began to hear the sound of someone saying aloud, 'Rama, Rama, Rama...', At first, he thought it was the sound of his own thoughts, which were forever remembering Rama. Then he realised that another voice outside was chanting his Lord's name. Hanuman moved towards the sound, and saw a small garden enclosing a house, In this garden, a temple had been built, where fresh flowers had been placed, and a lamp burnt inside.

Hanuman entered the garden by climbing down the wall that enclosed it. As he neared the temple, he saw a man sitting rapt, with closed eyes and folded hands, praying to Rama. Hanuman went close to the man, folded his own hands, and said, 'Jai Siya Ram!' by way of greeting. The man opened his eyes, and looked upon his visitor with some astonishment, This changed to friendliness when he heard Hanuman speak.

"Dear friend," began Hanuman. "You cannot imagine how happy you have made me this morning. I am thrilled to hear the name of my master, Sri Rama. I am Hanuman, Rama's messenger, and I have spent the night in search of Ma Sita, Please tell me who you are, and how you come to be praying to Rama."

The man bent down to touch Hanuman's feet. There were tears of happiness in his eyes. "My name is Vibhishan, and I am Ravana's brother," he said. "For a long time I have lived among my demon family, as a tongue has to live, surrounded by fearsome teeth. Only my love for Rama has been giving me strength. But today, I feel truly blessed. If God did not love me, He would not have presented me the company of good and saintly persons. By sending you here today, He has made me feel hopeful, for His trust and love. Tell me, can a demon like me ever hope to be counted as one of his devotees?"

"Dear Vibhishan," said Hanuman, touched by the sheer appeal of one of Rama's devotees. "You need never again have doubts such as these. Rama recognises love and devotion. Beyond this, it does not matter to him, whether you are high or low born, ugly or beautiful, intelligent or plain stupid, rich or poor. All he cares about is what you feel about him in your heart. Wherever he finds love, he blesses the one who feels it, in full measure. That is how kind he is, and that is why even a monkey like me, could have the rare good fortune of becoming his servant and messenger."

For some time, both Hanuman and Vibhishan spoke about Rama and the moments passed between them like the sipping of sweet nectar. But soon, Hanuman remembered his mission, and asked Vibhishan where Sita was.

"She is a prisoner in the beautiful, walled garden called Ashok Vatika," said Vibhishan. "This garden is guarded by Ravana's hand-picked sentries and soldiers. In the middle of this garden is a lake. On its banks there is a Shiva temple. Ma Sita sits under an Ashoka tree near this temple, and her condition is pitiable. My wife and eldest daughter Kala occasionally visit her to comfort her. Otherwise, she-demons from Ravana's court often go to taunt her, and try to force her into accepting Ravana's demands. Make your way to her with speed, I look forward to the day when Sri Rama will arrive here to liberate her!"

Alarmed by the picture Vibhishan had painted of Ma Sita's plight, Hanuman thanked him for his help, and went immediately to Ashok Vatika. Extremely cautious, he adopted his small form, and crept past all the guards, approaching the Ashoka tree under which Sita sat.

The sight that met his eyes was heart-rending. Sita sat, wearing a tattered saree, with no jewellery, except a small tiara on her forehead to show that she was a queen. Her hair hung limp, in a single plait clown her back, and her eyes were swollen from crying. Her face was gaunt, and her body looked frail and small. Even as Hanuman watched her, wondering how to introduce himself, Ravana arrived with his coterie of she-demons.

This was one of Ravana's morning visits to try and convince Sita to stop mourning for Rama, and consent to be his queen. He looked tall and threatening. A row of heads sprang out from either side of his normal, human head. He was called Dashanan, or the Ten-Headed One. Ravana's powers came out of his worship of Shiva. He considered himself to be unconquerable. But even though he used all manner of threats to frighten Sita, she still refused to give in to him. Laughing an arrogant laugh, Ravana demanded to know from Sita if she still expected to be rescued by her husband.

"Do not speak of my husband. You do not deserve to take his name. You are a mere firefly and he is the sun!" replied Sita, scornfully.

Her body looked weak, but her spirit had stayed strong.

The she-demons began jeering at Sita, and Ravana looked extremely annoyed by her words. "My patience is running out," he warned her. "If you have not consented to becoming my wife within a month, you can say goodbye to everything!"

Hanuman could hardly restrain himself from leaping at the cruel and arrogant Ravana. How he longed to crush Ravana and make him regret everything - his words, his deeds, even the fact that he was born! But that would be completed by Rama. Hanuman waited for Ravana and his coterie to leave. His job now was to bring some hope to Sita.

The brave show Sita had put up before Ravana crumbled after he had left. Consumed by sobs, Sita cried aloud. "What is the use of living like this, captured by this devil and subject to his evil mercy! He will surely kill me when this month is past. O gods in the heavens," said Sita looking up. "Can you not spare a spark for me to set myself aflame and die? O Ashoka tree! You see my misery daily. Spare me a dry branch, and a spark..."

Hanuman could not bear this trend of Sita's speech. From his hiding place, he threw the ring Rama had given him towards Sita.

Rama's royal ring, which Sita was most familiar with, suddenly rolled along the ground and stopped at Sita's feet. Sita picked it up, and was delighted to think that Rama was somehow near. She was curious about how the ring got there. She was flooded with hope – perhaps her ordeal was finally to end? Holding the ring to her heart with trembling fingers, Sita looked here and there for the person who could have dropped it.

Her eyes fell upon a small monkey figure, who stood before her with folded hands.

Hanuman had taken care not to appear too strange and strong to Sita, who had never seen him before. The last thing he wanted was to add to her fright and unhappiness. Now he spoke humbly, "Ma, it was I who threw the ring at your feet. I have carried it over the ocean with a message from my Lord, Sri Rama. He wished me to tell you to have courage till he arrives to free you from Ravana's clutches. He gave me the ring so you would know I am indeed coming from him."

Sita gazed at this monkey devotee of her husband. How strange he was, yet how comforting! Her face broke into a smile. "So you are the messenger who brought this! Come sit beside me and tell me everything. How did you become your master's helper? Where is he now?"

Happy to have brought the first sign of joy to Ma Sita's face, Hanuman sat at her feet and began relating the story of his meeting with Rama, and how the monkey and bear army had joined in searching for her.

The Ashok Vatika
Adventure

Sita was enthralled by Hanuman's description of how he had first had the fortune to meet Rama and Lakshman, how Sugreev and Rama had become friends, how the group of monkeys and bears had moved south in search of her and how Sampaati the vulture had guided them to Lanka.

Hanuman was happy to see her face lighting up with hope. Since she had received news of Rama there seemed to be a renewed strength in her. While Hanuman told her the whole story he did not make much of his own fearless actions. While he spoke Sita gazed in wonder at this small monkey figure with the slightly crooked chin (Hanuman's chin had been bent a little out of shape when Indra s thunderbolt had struck him)

When Hanuman described the vast monkey and bear army that stood ready to fight alongside Rama with the demons of Lanka, Sita laughed softly.

Hanuman was surprised by her laugh, and looked enquiringly at her. She explained, "Dear son, you are full of courage, and your love for Sri Rama is clear to anyone. But are you sure that you can fight the hundreds of hefty, well-armed rakshasas in Ravana's army? Are all the monkeys and bears in Sugreev's army as small as you are?"

When he heard this, Hanuman understood that the time had come to show her his true form. Bowing his head, and folding his hands, he said, "Ma, I did not want to frighten you. Permit me to make my true form known to you." He took a few deep breaths and grew taller than several of the trees that grew around them!

Sita looked up at a tall and powerful monkey who looked fully capable of lifting whole chariots and their horses up into the air! He yawned soundlessly, and Sita got a glimpse of his fearsome teeth, while he stretched his arms to reveal sharp nails on his hands. When he finally turned his golden-brown eyes on her again, she looked satisfied.

"There are many other warriors like me in our army," Hanuman assured Sita.

"But none can be as devoted to my husband," Sita said with a smile, making Hanuman very happy. Reminded of Rama, Sita sighed and asked, "Tell me, does my husband think of me, or has he busied himself with other things?"

"Ma!" cried out Hanuman. "Every moment spent separated from you seems like an age to Rama. You are in his thoughts every waking moment, and he is only waiting for the moment when he can free you. He has asked me to pray to you to be patient till he is able to destroy Ravana and his kingdom, and take you back home!"

Sita looked definitely happier now that she could see an end to her agony. "I am waiting for that moment with all my heart and soul. But you heard what that demon said to me. If I should still refuse to be his queen at the end of this month, he will destroy me. So return to my husband as soon as you can, and help him in his task."

Hanuman bent to touch Sita's feet. She placed her hand on his head, and said, "You have brought me much comfort and hope. You are selfless, and intelligent, and extremely brave. May no power on earth destroy you! May you always be beloved of Sri Rarna!"

These words of blessing had a powerful effect on Hanuman. His eyes shining, he said, "Ma, thank you for your blessings! You can move the gods in the heavens with your prayers. Your support is very valuable to me. After hearing your words, every last fear about completing my task has left me."

In his happiness, Hanuman did a small dance - he leapt with joy, and swished his tail, while Sita watched in some amusement. Then he stood before her once again. "Ma, I have been travelling, and awake all night. I am hungry, and notice there are choice fruits all around us in this garden. If you permit me, I would like to eat some of these and satisfy my hunger."

"Go ahead and eat what you need, dear Hanuman. But remember, this garden is heavily guarded by Ravana's most fierce soldiers," said Sita.

Hanuman leapt on to a tree branch and plucked a ripe fruit. He feasted on tropical Lankan delicacies like rambutans and mangosteen. He also found jackfruit, guava, mango, banana, citrus fruits and chikoos to satisfy his hunger,

It was while he ate that it occurred to him, that this would be a valuable chance to test Ravana's army. How could he encounter Ravana's guards and soldiers? Thinking this, Hanuman's behavior underwent a change. He began throwing about half-eaten fruit. He began uprooting trees, flinging their branches far and wide, He sniffed at bushes as if he was searching for some choice fruit, then threw them to join the green branches in heaps.

Very soon, the Ashok Vatika began to resemble a battle scene.

The only tree left undamaged was the one under which Sita sat. A large number of gardeners, guards and soldiers came rushing up to ask Hanuman to stop his destruction immediately. But these demons did not know what hit them. Each received a blow that made him fly into the air, then come down to the ground with a loud thud.

The temple in the midst of the Ashok Vatika was a beautiful building called 'Chaitya Praasaad'. Hanuman jumped on top of this building, and surveyed the damage he had done. The terrified demons sent messengers to Ravana in his court.

"A huge monkey has appeared out of nowhere, and is destroying Ashok Vatika!" these excited messengers informed Ravana. This disturbed Ravana much more than he could reveal to his courtiers.

This was because, that morning, before he had woken up, he had been dreaming about a giant monkey making his life miserable. Also, his wife Mandodari had told him about the warnings of an old she-demon named Trijata. Trijata had said that Ravana should immediately return Sita to her husband with honour. If he failed to do so, it would lead to the complete destruction of the Lanka demons at the hands of monkeys and bears! So Ravana was already beginning to look askance at monkeys.

One of Ravana's generals, Jambumali, was summoned, and Ravana said to him, "Go and destroy this monkey, and bring his corpse to me."

Instead, they carried in a dead Jambumali, not half an hour later, into Ravana's court,

To the demons who went to challenge him, Hanuman now presented a truly terrible sight. All the hair on his body was standing on end, making him look even larger than he was. His face had turned an angry red, and his expression was completely fierce. Every few minutes, he stopped and emitted a thunderous roar that shook the Ashok Vatika, and reached the ears of Ravana's courtiers in the palace far away.

Lacking weapons in the face of the heavily armed soldiers sent by Ravana, Hanuman had armed himself with the stone pillars of the Chaitya Praasaad. He had destroyed this building and sat perched on the ruins. The huge pillars were like his own personal battering arms, and the demons just scattered before this attack.

Jambumali's death made Ravana send his son Akshakumar to capture Hanuman. "I rely on you to kill this threat to Lanka, son," said Ravana. Akshakumar set off with many soldiers and much fanfare.

The grief and wailing that greeted the news of his death was even louder than the farewell he had received hours earlier.

Eyewitnesses said the monkey had swooped down from the sky on Ravana's son, and carried him away to a great height, from where he was flung down to the ground. Hearing this, Ravana felt the sharp pangs of fear, in addition to his grief at losing a son. For a few moments, he did not know what to do.

Then his son Meghnaad, who had once defeated Indra, the king of the gods, in battle, and received the name Indrajit, offered to go and capture Hanuman.

Ravana had no option except to permit his eldest and most beloved son to go and confront this menace. But he put a word of caution in Meghnaad's ear. "Use your ultimate weapon if you have to. This is no ordinary monkey."

When Meghnaad arrived with additional members of Ravana's army to the garden, he was truly taken aback by the scene that met his eyes. Hanuman leaped to great heights, then jumped from these on to Meghnaad's soldiers, swinging his heavy stone pillars from both arms. The injured and battered soldiers began to pile up around Meghnaad.

He let fly dozens of arrows from his bow at Hanuman. Some of these deadly missiles hurt Hanuman, and his blood began to flow, but he continued to fight with the same ferocity.

Extremely rattled and fearful, Meghnaad decided to use the 'Brahma Shaap', a powerful mantra that had the effect of paralysing the person on whom it was used. Now Hanuman was in a strange dilemma. As a baby, Brahma had blessed him that all the weapons Brahma had created would have no effect on Hanuman. So he was free to continue to fight, if he wished.

But such a powerful mantra has to be shown respect, otherwise ordinary people will lose faith in the powers of the gods.

So Hanuman decided to surrender to the Brahma Shaap. He lay still while Meghnaad's demon assistants tied him up securely with thick ropes made out of twisted vines. What Meghnaad's assistants did not know, is that the Brahma Shaap paralysis is negated if any other method is used to restrain the person who is under its effect. By tying up Hanuman, after he was paralysed, Meghnaad's assistants were effectively freeing him from the same paralysis!

Hanuman began to move under the knotted vines, and Meghnaad got worried when he saw this. He realised that the Brahma Shaap had worn off, and could not be used again on the same person. He wondered at the power of this strange monkey who had appeared as if from nowhere, and destroyed his father's treasured garden.

Hanuman's tied figure was led through the streets of Lanka to be taken to Ravana's court. A great crowd of curious Lanka citizens had collected to see the monkey who had done such damage before he was captured. As Hanuman passed in the streets, these people shouted and jeered at him, or pinched and cuffed him as he passed. None of this abuse and violence seemed to disturb Ramdoot. He was calm and dignified in the custody of the demons. While the Lankans taunted him, his eyes darted to and fro, noticing the city's roads, alleys, buildings and landmarks. The previous night, Hanuman had not been able to notice as much in the darkness as he would have liked to.

Now he noted every aspect of the city that Rama would soon attack.

Even in the most difficult circumstances, Hanuman never lost sight of his task, nor the means to bring it to success.

The Power of
Hanuman's Tail

Tied, bruised and surrounded by guards, Hanuman stood in Ravana's court, and gazed upon the king of Lanka. He looked calm, and his powerful brain was noting a great many things.

Ravana sat on a sparkling throne, made of the glacier stone called 'sphatika'. His clothes were dazzling, and every one of his heads had a crown of a different style and design. These crowns were studded with hundreds of bright, coloured gems. His moustache increased the fierceness of his expression.

As Ravana and Hanuman stared at each other, Hanuman was thinking, 'If this powerful king had chosen the path of goodness, rather than that of wrongdoing, how great he could have been! But alas!

There is only one possible fate for him now - to be defeated and killed by my Lord.'

Meghnaad addressed his father, "Here is my brother's murderer and the destroyer of Ashok Vatika. Hundreds of our bravest soldiers, and some of our distinguished generals have died at his hands. I have brought him here so you may know from him why he did what he has done."

Ravana's brow was black as thunder. He spoke in a deep and rumbling voice, "You look like a monkey, but you have caused so much destruction! Who are you? What made you kill so many of my men, and destroy my garden?"

Completely unafraid, even though his hands were tied, Hanuman looked at Ravana and said, "I am the messenger of him whose wife you brought by force to Lanka. I have crossed the sea to see that she is safe. Rama's message to you is to return her immediately, or face the terrible consequences."

"A messenger!" exclaimed Ravana, "Ha! That's a tall claim. If you are a mere messenger, why did you wreak such havoc? Was that part of your duty?"

"And your message?" he continued. " Do you seriously believe that I can pay heed to the words of a monkey, and bow down to the whims of Rama? I have no such intention!" thundered Ravana.

"O Ravana, king of Lanka, you are right, I am a monkey. But I have the great good fortune of being in the service of God Himself! My Lord, Sri Rama is the sworn protector of all living creatures. His strength, bravery, love and kindness is known throughout the world.

Don't you remember? He is that son of King Dasharath, who lifted and accidentally broke the mighty bow of Shiva, that you could not even move in Raja Janak's court! He killed the demons Khar-Dushan and Trishira, single-handed, along with fourteen thousand of their rakshasa friends! My Lord is God in human form. He lives on earth to protect the meek, the innocent, and the good."

Ravana was growing angrier with every passing moment that Hanuman spoke.

Hanuman continued in a quieter tone, "O king, you are most powerful, but you would do well to remember this. There is not a single creature who can get away after having wronged my Lord.

He metes out justice to every evil doer. Yet, he also has the kindest heart, and is quick to forgive. If you should return Ma Sita to him, and ask for his forgiveness, he will surely have mercy on you. It is not for nothing that he is called "Bhaktavatsal" or parent of all who pray to him!"

Ravana opened his mouth and his words came out in a roar, "How dare you advise me to fall at Rama's feet? I shall die before I do such a thing!."

Hanuman smiled, and continued to give sage words of advice to Ravana. "Today you seem unbeatable, surrounded by power, prestige and riches," he said. "But life is strange indeed. Nothing lasts here – the body grows old, riches are spent or lose their shine, people change their affections and loyalties. All that you are trying to hold on to, is bound to leave you. It is only the love for God that will help you to cross the bridge from this world to the next. Surrender to Sri Rama before it is too late!"

Ravana could not bear to hear any more. Red-faced and raging, he called to his guards to grab Hanuman and put him to death.

At this, Vibhishan, who had been watching the whole scene with great agitation, stepped forward and said, "Respected brother, even if this messenger has made you most angry, we must not forget that he is indeed a messenger. Ethics do not permit us to kill a messenger, whether in war, or in peace!"

This timely advice made Ravana pause, then his face broke into an ugly sneer. "I have the perfect remedy for this monkey's gross insolence," he said. "Monkeys are very fond of their tails - much of their beauty depends on these. Set fire to Hanuman's tail. That will teach him to try and cow me down." With this, he raised his head and laughed a loud demonic laugh.

Meghnaad and his assistants took Hanuman outside and began tying oil-soaked cloth rags around his tail. Hanuman did not protest, or struggle. Instead, he made his tail grow longer so that more rags, oil, and ghee had to be brought. The tail grew longer and longer, and the people gathering to see the tail getting burnt, had to struggle to bring more and more materials.

So many rags were brought, so much oil and ghee poured onto the ever growing tail, that suddenly, a shortage of these materials began to be felt in Lanka. At last, the tail was bound tight with the burning materials to everyone's satisfaction.

Hanuman had stopped making it grow. He now sat, looking bored. A she-demon rushed to the spot where Sita sat, and breathlessly told her, "The monkey who was seen speaking to you this morning has been captured and his tail is going to be set alight!"

Sita was shocked and an exclamation left her lips, "O God please protect Ramdoot! Do not let these demons harm him!" Unable to rush to Hanuman's side, Sita sat down and began to pray.

With a demonic laugh, Meghnaad picked up a flaming torch and set fire to Hanuman's tail. For a few moments, Hanuman sat, with tied hands, and looked upon the scene. Thousands of jeering and screaming Lankan citizens were waiting expectantly for him to burn before their eyes.

Silently, Hanuman closed his eyes, and inwardly said, 'Jai Siya Ram!' then, with the tip of his tail flaming with fire, he made himself very small and slipped out of the thick ropes which bound him.

Freed from the ropes, hanuman jumped up onto a building and swished his long tail. The elaborate structure caught fire, and the people who had gathered to watch began to gasp. For the first time, they began to feel alarmed, and began to scatter as the flames leapt out of the burning building.

Sita prayed to Agni, the god of fire to turn cool for Hanuman. Agni had promised never to harm Hanuman when he was still an infant. The flames turned cool for Hanuman alone.

Ramdoot looked at his burning tail and thought, 'Strange that these leaping flames should feel cool against my skin!' Then he thought of Sita. 'I am sure Ma is praying for my safety,' he decided. 'Jai Siyaram!'

From this moment there was no stopping Hanuman. Ever agile, he leapt from rooftop to rooftop, setting fire to the homes of generals, the granary, mint, stables and storehouses of the kingdom of Lanka. The people who had been screaming for his blood just moments earlier now screamed in panic and ran helter-skelter. They tried to save their belongings, holding their children to their breasts. From time to time, Hanuman roared in sheer abandon – a very loud and frightening sound that did full justice to one of his names – Mahabalaaya or the Mighty One.

He moved so fast that he seemed to be everywhere at once. While Meghnaad and his courtiers saw him set one building aflame, it seemed as if he was in another building the very next instant. Vayu, the god of wind, began to help Hanuman by blowing hot and gusty winds. These magnified the effect of the flames, making them spread speedily from one building to another. The great golden kingdom of Lanka was being razed to the ground. All because of the terrible fury of a messenger of God whom Ravana had made the mistake of thinking a mere monkey.

At the end of it, only one house remained standing untouched in Lanka. This was the home of Vibhishan with the words 'Jai Sri Ram' painted on the threshold. Hanuman reached the shore and used the sea water to put out the flames of his tail. He leaned for a moment over the waters, exhausted and dripping with sweat. Then he thought of Sita, and went leaping and scampering to where she sat, extremely worried about him.

He fell at her feet, and she patted his head. She said, "I have been so worried about you. Thank God you are safe!"

Hanuman looked at her with shining eyes. "It was your prayers that protected me, Ma," he said. He continued, still aware of his task, "I must leave now. Do give me permission to leave, Ma. I must reach Rama and let him know how you are. Please await our earliest return, and stay strong!"

Sita's tears flowed at his words, but she smiled and said farewell. "Your coming here gave me much strength. I have no doubt at all that you shall soon return with your master."

Hanuman said, "Your days of suffering will soon end forever. For now, please give me something of your own to give Rama. That will bring him solace, just as his ring brought comfort to you."

Sita removed the small tiara from her head that was the last remaining piece of her royal jewellery. She gave this to Hanuman and said, "Tell him to hurry!"

Then she placed her hand on Hanuman's head one last time. "You are like a beloved son to me. I pray you succeed in every mission!"

Hanuman turned away to return to Kishkindha where Sugreev, Rama and Lakshman awaited word of Sita. As he prepared to leave, the flames that his tail had spread around Lanka continued to leap up into the sky at several places. The citizens of Lanka had learned the hard way just what power resided in Ramdoots tail.

Hanuman's Great Good Fortune

Ramdoot was greatly lifted by his meeting with Sita and his adventures in Lanka. He looked forward to the moment when he would be able to tell Rama that he had met Sita. He passed over the ocean once more, briefly touching the peak of Mainaak, as if in salute,

Angad, Jambavant and the other monkeys had heard Hanuman's mighty roar all the way across the ocean, when he had burnt Lanka.

They were now in a state of excited anticipation. "Such a mighty sound can only mean that our brave friend has defeated the rakshasas," said wise Jambavant. "I am sure we are about to get news of Ma Sita," said Angad, expressing everybody's faith in Hanuman.

Hanuman appeared over the horizon, and arrived in their midst.

What a merry scene it was! Monkey friends rushed to touch him and greet him. Hanuman patted some of them on the back, hugged others, and let some of them have the pleasure of riding on his back! Everyone was chattering all at once, delighted with his safe return. After a while, the group became serious again, and sat around Angad, to discuss what to do.

When Hanuman described meeting Sita, the group set up a happy cheer. When he spoke about being captured, their eyes grew round and anxious. When he described Ravana ordering his tail to be burnt, the monkeys gasped and said 'Oooh!' A few even clutched their own tails in alarm. But moments later, when Hanuman related what had happened with the burning tail, they were leaping about and shouting.

At the end of the story, Angad took a few steps forward and gripped Hanuman by the shoulders. "We are all grateful to you, Hanuman! You have made it possible for us to face Rama, Lakshman, and King Sugreev again. Where would we be if we had failed in the task set for us? Let us now return to Kishkindha armed with this happy news!"

Boosted by their friend's success, the group of monkeys and bears departed for Kishkindha. Their progress was swift, and they entered the kingdom of Kishkindha a few days later. The enticing garden of Madhuvan, where ripe and delicious fruits grew, came in their path.

These fruits were guarded by an old monkey warrior named Dadhimukh, who was Sugreev's uncle. The happy monkeys returning from their southern journey were all thirsting for the juice of the Madhuvan fruits. They looked at Angad, and at a nod of approval from him, they began feasting, unworried by Dadhimukh's shouts of anger.

The sweet juice of the Madhuvan fruits went straight to the monkeys' heads. They began dancing, leaping from tree to tree, and expressing their happiness in a hundred different ways. They put their arms around each other's shoulders, and began singing loud monkey songs. Some jumped up and down and bared their teeth at Dadhimukh when he arrived to shout at them.

The old monkey raced to inform Sugreev, who was staying with Rama and Lakshman on the peak of Prasravangiri mountain, where Rama lived in a hut made from forest leaves. A seat had been carved on a glittering sphatika boulder, for the two brothers from Ayodhya, and Sugreev himself attended on them.

Dadhimukh arrived and indignantly narrated how the monkey band had returned with Angad and Hanuman, and they were showing scant respect for his authority, eating the Madhuvan fruits at will.

This news, far from upsetting Sugreev, caused him to smile and look at Rama and Lakshman, "I am sure Hanuman has achieved the task we had set for him," he said. "The monkeys would never dare to eat the Madhuvan fruits, if they had not been extremely happy. Even though the time of one month we had set for them is over, their happiness seems to spell their success."

Just as Sugreev spoke, Hanuman, Angad and Jambavant arrived and stood before Rama with folded hands, waiting to meet him.

"Welcome back," said Sugreev. "Your companions' behaviour leads us to think that your mission was successful! Speak, and tell us, did you succeed in finding the whereabouts of Ma Sita?"

Ramdoot stood with folded hands looking straight at Rama. He said, "I had the fortune to meet Ma Sita in Lanka."

These simple words had a powerful effect on Rama. "You met her? How is she? Is she well? Come here, sit down and tell me about your meeting." At this invitation Hanuman sat down at Rama s feet.

He said, "She is kept in the garden named Ashok Vatika. There she sits alone under an Ashoka tree. She is agonised in spirit. Rakshasis torment and tease her and Ravana arrives occasionally to force her to submit to his demands. She resists everything with great courage. Her clothes are torn, she wears her hair in a single plait down her back and she breathes your name with every breath. She looks gaunt and weak. All that keeps her alive is the hope that you will soon arrive to rescue her from the clutches of Ravana."

The word picture that Hanuman had drawn worried Rama immensely. Hanuman took the tiara that Ma Sita had given him, and gave it to Rama. "Ma asked me to give you this, and said to tell you to hurry, as Ravana has threatened to force her to submit to him in a month's time."

Rama looked at the tiara as if it was the most precious object in the universe. "This is the 'Chudamani' that my father in law had received from the gods. He gave it to beloved Sita on our wedding day. I have always seen it adorning her head. Now it reminds me of what she is going through."

Rama stood up and lifted Hanuman with a hand on each of his shoulders. He looked into his friend s eyes and his own were brimming with gratitude. "You have proved how impossible it is for me to ever repay you

Hanuman!" he said. "I thank you from the bottom of my heart!"

With these words Rama moved forward and enveloped Hanuman in a great embrace. The universe spun around Hanuman. It was as if a lightning bolt of energy had entered his monkey frame and his breath was knocked out of him.

Then Rama's love took hold of him and under its healing effect, he began sobbing like a baby. At this moment it was clear that Rama was accepting Hanuman as a part of Himself, without any reserve.

When he was released, Hanuman clutched his master's feet and refused to let go. In vain did Rama pat his head, and try to lift him up. Hanuman stayed where he was, crying, "Rama! Protect me. Never leave me for an instant. I am nothing without you." It was some more time before he was calm enough to speak again.

"What did you find out about Lanka? Could you see how strong Ravana's army is?" Lakshman asked Hanuman. Ramdoot related the story of what happened in Lanka. When he saw the admiration on the faces of his listeners, as he spoke about the burning of Lanka, he suddenly paused. Once more reaching down to touch Rama's feet, he said, "Whatever I did in Lanka was only possible because you had trusted me, blessed me, given me strength and courage. It was all your doing, I could never have done it without you."

Rama smiled at the modesty and devotion of Rambhakt. Losing no more time, the entire assembly prepared to leave immediately for Lanka to rescue Ma Sita. The information given to them by Hanuman would prove invaluable in their mission,

The foundation for Rama's victory over Ravana was laid by Hanuman.

Sanjivani Heals

Rama's army reached the Lankan shore for a fierce war with Ravana. Accompanied by Sugreev with his thousands of bears and monkeys, Rama, Lakshman and Hanuman fought the might of Ravana's warriors and weapons. They had crossed over to Lanka from India by building a bridge of floating rocks. Each day, the battle grew bigger, the fighting more intense.

For Ravana, his son Meghnaad was a very important fighter.

Meghnaad not only had a knowledge of powerful mantras for victory in battle, he was also very cunning. He remembered that Hanuman was a formidable foe, since the burning of Lanka, Thus, he avoided any direct fighting with Hanuman. Instead, he attacked the large numbers of soldiers of the monkey army, whom he terrorised with his sharp arrows. One such attack troubled the monkey army so much that they rushed to Hanuman for help.

Hanuman was so angry that he did not pause to pick up proper weapons. He just lifted an entire hill that was situated nearby, and flung this at Meghnaad. But Meghnaad managed to escape getting crushed under this strange missile. Hundreds of rakshasa soldiers came under the hill.

Lakshman and Meghnaad were deadly enemies. One day, when they were fighting intensely, Lakshman succeeded in destroying Meghnaad's chariot. Meghnaad had to run across the battlefield littered with the bodies of dead rakshasas. Hotly pursued by Lakshman, Meghnaad decided to use the most powerful 'Amogh Shakti', a gift from Brahma that no enemy could withstand. He put this shakti to his arrow, and aimed at Lakshman, who was gaining on him. The Shakti pierced Lakshman's chest. He fell from his chariot, with blood oozing out of the deep wound the arrow had created. The wound was so lethal that Lakshman became unconscious, his life hanging by a slender thread.

Meghnaad rushed to pick Lakshman up. He wanted to carry him away as proof of his major victory. But however hard he heaved and tried, he could not make Lakshman move by an inch, Meanwhile the monkey soldiers around Lakshman had rushed to Hanuman.

They told him of what had happened to Lakshman, and he came immediately to Lakshman's side. Meghnaad had fled, sensing that Hanuman would soon arrive on the scene.

The sight of Lakshman bleeding and lying absolutely still filled Hanuman with dread. Lakshman's face was streaked with mud and blood. For an instant, Hanuman looked at the retreating soldiers of Meghnaad and Ravana's army and his eyes seemed to be shooting angry flames. Then he roared and made them scurry away faster. He did not pursue them knowing that he should first attend to Lakshman.

He lifted Lakshman with ease and carried him tenderly to where Rama was waiting in a worried state. Rama was shocked to see his brother in a wounded and unconscious state. He asked immediately for a doctor to be brought to tend to his brother. When he heard that the wound had been caused by Brahma's weapon he grew very angry.

"Meghnaad should be made to pay for what he has done," declared Rama. "But first how are we to bring Lakshman to consciousness?"

Everyone huddled together and Vibhishan revealed that there was a very good doctor in Lanka named Sushen. "If he could be brought here he would surely know how to cure Lakshman," said Vibhishan.

This was enough for Hanuman to act. Taking a minute to note Sushen's address, Rambhakt left immediately. He approached Lanka in his tiny insect form. When he reached Sushen's home, he decided to lift him up, house and all, and carry him to the battlefield. He did not want to waste time in explaining the whole situation to the doctor and was also worried that Sushen would refuse to come.

So he lifted up the physician s house with him inside it and carried it with all speed to where Lakshman lay. Sushen stepped outside his door and was amazed to find himself in a battlefield instead of his own courtyard. He was a good doctor and did not protest at being asked to treat someone who was an enemy of Lanka. He felt Lakshman's pulse, examined his wound, then looked up at the setting sun. "There is one herb that can cure this condition," he said. "But it is only found in the far North on the slopes of the Dronachal mountain that stands between the peaks of Kailash and Rishabh. This mountain has many magical herbs Vishalyakarini, Suvarnakarini, Sandhani and Sanjivani. It is Sanjivani that I need before sunrise, to tend to this wound. If this is not brought before dawn, it will become impossible to save Sri Lakshman."

These words struck a chill in the hearts of all those who heard them. Hanuman saw his beloved Rama's face turn pale. He went close to Rama, and asked, "How

can this be, O Lord? How can you be separated from
your beloved brother by the shadow of Death? Shall I
challenge Death to a fight, and finish him forever? By
doing thus, I shall not only be bringing your brother
back, but also relieving all living creatures from the
fear of death forever!"

Rama could not help but smile at Hanuman's
determination. "You speak like one with great powers,
and that is natural," he said. "But remember that God
works within the natural world by observing the laws
of nature. If I were to let you defeat Death for my
sake, how could my life be a lesson for human beings?
While I stay in this body, I must endure the pain it
suffers."

"Then I shall leave immediately, to bring back
Saniivani," said Hanuman. "Even a moment's delay
may prove fatal now." With the words "Jai Siyaram!"
on his lips, he raised his hands skywards, and was soon
a distant speck in the sky.

Travelling at the speed of a meteor, Hanuman
reached the foothills of the Himalayas, where he felt
very thirsty. He could see a beautiful forest ashrarn or
'tapovan' in which a sadhu sat meditating. Hanuman
approached the sadhu, and said, 'Respected muni, I
have travelled very far, and am thirsty. Please direct
me to the nearest source of water."

The muni opened his eyes and smiled. "Welcome, son," he said. "You may drink the water in my 'kamandal' (sadhu's special vessel)."

"Such a small quantity of water will not satisfy me, dear sir," said Hanuman. "Please direct me to a lake or river."

"Why do you look so worried?" questioned the sadhu, with a strange smile. "I have the gift of seeing past, present and future, and I can see that you are Hanuman, Rama's messenger, come here to obtain medicine for Rama's brother Lakshman. I can also see that he is now recovered. You need not hurry and worry. Drink water, eat some fruits, rest here and return in the morning."

This strange sadhu was actually the rakshasa Kaalnemi. He had been placed as an obstacle in Hanuman's path by Ravana. It was his plan to somehow keep Hanuman from returning to the battlefield with the healing herb.

But Hanuman was not so easily fooled. He said with firmness, "I thank you for your kind offer, sage. But I cannot rest till I have seen my Lord's face again, and I will not stop till I have done what he needs me to do."

Kaalnemi saw that if he asked Hanuman to stay till morning, he risked being discovered. So he cleverly said, "Very well. The herb that you are seeking grows on a mountain which shines in the dark because of its medicinal powers. Newcomers find it very hard to recognise the herb from among the rest. I shall give you some secret mantras by which you can find the true Sanjivani. Meanwhile, go to the lake behind this ashram and satisfy your thirst. And remember, do not open your eyes under any circumstance as you drink the water!"

Hanuman bowed and made no comment about these strange instructions. Then he went to the lake, closed his eyes, and bending low, began to sip the water. A movement near him made him open his eyes. He saw a huge, monstrous fish before him, preparing to swallow him whole.

In a flash, he understood that this was the reason the sadhu had sent him to drink with his eyes closed, He must have wanted Hanuman to be eaten by the fish.

Before he had time to think further, Hanuman's hand had shot out and snatched at the fish in such a way that its' huge body split into two. To his horror Hanuman saw the dead body of the fish come floating to the surface. But at the same time, an apsara appeared briefly in the sky above him.

The ethereal creature smiled at Hanuman and said, "Dear Hanuman, I am Dhanyamali, an apsara who was cursed to live in the body of a fish till you liberated me." As Hanuman continued to gaze up at her, she went on, "Beware of the sadhu who sent you here. He is Kaalnemi, a rakshasa and great friend of Ravana's. He will do everything in his power to prevent you from doing your duty unless you figure out a way to get rid of him first." She then smiled and disappeared into the sky.

Hanuman returned to the sadhu with a grim look on his face. Kaalnemi welcomed him and said, "You had your drink of water? Come, now sit by me and receive 'deeksha' (the teaching of a guru). I will teach you how to recognise the special herb Sanjivani."

With puja materials spread out before him, Kaalnemi thought that he could while away the entire night in teaching Hanuman many elaborate rituals and mantras. But Mahabalaya had other ideas.

"Before I take deeksha, let me offer you my guru dakshina (teacher's fee)," said Hanuman. Saying this he picked up Kaalnemi with a single hand and flung him high in the sky. From this height, he must have surely fallen and crashed to the ground but there was no trace of him after that. Hanuman continued towards the Kailash and Rishabh mountains.

Soon he stood before the peaks, wrth Dronachal visible between the two majestic mountains. But the

Kaalnemi episode had left its mark on Hanuman. He had forgotten the name and description of Sanjivani!

Now he looked up at the mountain and scratched his head. The mountain truly glittered with its magical 'Maha Aushadhis' (miraculous medicines). Then Hanuman was struck by a thought. Why not carry the whole mountain back with him? That way there was no danger that he was leaving behind anything important.

To think was to act, and he scooped out the medicine mountain and held it up in his left hand. His right hand still held the golden mace or 'gada' that was his signature weapon against evildoers. This he rested on his right shoulder.

Poised like this, he soared through the night sky, the huge mountain covered with trees and bushes making a whooshing sound as it passed through the air. Hanuman had only one thought in mind - to reach the magical herb to Sushen before it was too late.

As Hanuman passed over Ayodhya, he was spotted by Bharat, Rama's brother, who was waiting for the days to pass when he would meet Rama again. Bharat thought the strange sight up above may be a demon who could be a threat to Ayodhya. Picking up an arrow without a sharp point, he lightly cast this into the sky, and brought Hanuman down.

For some moments, Hanuman lost consciousness, with the words 'Jai Shri Ram' on his lips.

Bharat heard this, and was amazed. This was his beloved elder brother's name. Could he have made the unpardonable mistake of hurting someone dear to Rama? Bharat anxiously watched Hanuman lying on the ground. When Hanuman did not revive, he silently prayed, 'O God, I have always had the purest love for my brother, but fate has snatched him away from me. Now fate seems to have played another cruel trick. If I am a true devotee of God, then let this flying monkey with the mountain become well again.'

Hanuman opened his eyes and saw a dark figure next to him with his hair in a top knot, dressed in simple clothes. Bharat had stopped wearing royal clothes and wore the same clothes his brothers and sister-in-law must be wearing in the forest. In his slightly dazed state, Hanuman thought this was Rama himself! He bent forward to touch Bharat's feet, and said, "I have brought the medicine for Lakshman, my Lord."

Bharat lifted Hanuman up with a hand on each shoulder.

"Esteemed visitor, you speak of Rama and Lakshman, and I yearn to have news of them! You must be their friend, and I am Bharat, their brother. This is Ayodhya, where I live, just waiting for the moment when I can see them again."

"Ayodhya!" exclaimed Hanuman. He bent low to kiss the earth. "Then this is the place my Lord always speaks of! And you are the brother whom he loves so much that you are never far from his thoughts."

"Is that so? Can it be thus?" wondered Bharat. "I always imagined that I am the most unfortunate man alive, to have been the cause of my beloved brother's exile! But do not speak of me. Tell me, why does Lakshman need medicine? How are Rama and he, and respected Janaki?"

Hanuman told him why he was there, and Bharat was more anguished than ever. He cried, "How cruel can fate be to me? Not only am I separated from my brothers, but I am also guilty of harming their friend and saviour. Can life be any worse?"

Moved by Bharat's agony, Hanuman consoled him as best as he could. "You are most beloved to Rama," he assured him. "Why, when he wants to express his affection for me, he says, 'You are as dear to me as Bharat is!'"

By now, several Ayodhya citizens had gathered to witness the strange scene. Before Hanuman knew what was happening, he was surrounded by Rama's family, with each one of them, particularly Rama's mother Kaushalya and Lakshman's mother Sumitra eager to have news about their near ones. Hanuman answered their questions as best as he could, but he was getting worried about precious moments passing without his mission being completed.

Bharat sensed this and quieted the others. "It has been wonderful to have news of our loved ones from you, dear Hanuman. But you must now leave to help heal Lakshman. Please permit me to help you. I will seat you on my fastest arrow and reach you straight to Rama."

Hanuman was about to open his mouth and ask how a single arrow could bear his weight, and a mountain's, but he remembered how a mild hit from Bharat's blunt arrow had brought him down to Ayodhya. So he said nothing, and gratefully accepted Bharat's help.

He understood that in the present situation, God's will was helping them along, making things happen in strange and wondrous ways.

Meanwhile Rama was extremely worried on behalf of all who loved him. "How could I fail to protect Lakshman, who left everything, to be with me? How will I face his mother and his wife, if I have to return to Ayodhya alone? I have failed to rescue my dear wife, who suffers endless misery with my name on her lips. How will I rescue her without Lakshman by my side? What about Vibhishan? If I should lose heart now, and this evil rakshasa conquers me, where will Vibhishan go? He can never return to Lanka if Ravana is king. Why have I been the cause of the ruin of so many lives?"

In the midst of all these gloomy thoughts, Hanuman arrived, bearing the glittering, magical burden of Dronachal. Sushen immediately set to work with the Sanjivani, and under the eyes of everyone present, Lakshman's chest wound healed. He began to stir, and in a few moments, opened his eyes and sat up.

True to his fiery, hot-blooded nature, Lakshman immediately looked around and said, "Where's Meghnaad?" It was as if his near-brush with death had never happened!

Hanuman could not help smiling. This was the sweetest reward for his pains.

He lifted Sushen and his house and placed it hack in its corner of Lanka. Before the rays of dawn had begun to creep across the sky, Hanuman had even restored the Dronachal mountain to its rightful place.

When it came to the service of Rama, there was no task too difficult or too tedious for Hanuman. He only thought of serving his master.

Ahiravan Fails In His Mission

The fierce war raging between Rama and Ravana and their respective armies, continued towards its inevitable end - Ravana's defeat. Every day, hundreds of Ravana's soldiers were dying in battle.

But when Lakshman had killed his beloved son Meghnaad, whom he thought was undefeatable, Ravana fell into a faint.

When he recovered, he became deeply depressed. He wondered how he was to continue fighting Rama, Lakshman, Hanuman, and their extremely brave and agile warriors led by Jambavant. It seemed as if no power on earth could stop them, and his defeat and death were certain. However, he decided to approach the demon king Ahiravan, who ruled over the underworld (or 'patal lok') for a miracle.

But how was he to find him, and call upon him for help? Ravana remembered that Ahiravan was a great worshipper of Devi, or Shakti. He decided to pray in the temple of the goddess and enlist Ahiravan's aid.

Ravana sat and meditated in the Devi temple and called upon Ahiravan. Soon the immense fearsome form of the demon king stood before him.

"Why have you remembered me?" asked Ahiravan tersely.

"O friend I find myself staring death in the face. King Dasharath's two sons Rama and Lakshman had been exiled to the forest. My sister Shurpanakha encountered them and wanted to marry Lakshman. In reply she had her ears and nose cut off. I wanted revenge and abducted Rama's wife Sita. Now they are camped at my doorstep, daily destroying huge chunks of my army. They have killed Meghnaad as well as mighty Kumbhakarna..." Ravana's eyes were filling with tears of self-pity.

"Hmm..." said Ahiravan, without much sympathy. "Lakshman was already married when he met your sister. What did you expect him to do? Besides, if you wanted revenge, it would have been better to challenge the two princes to a fight rather than make off with

Rama's wife. That is a very wrong, cowardly, and unjust thing to do." The demon king was certainly not mincing his words.

"Be that as it may, dear cousin," said Ravana in an apologetic voice, "I still need your help in this desperate situation."

"What do you want me to do?" asked Ahiravan.

"Take Rama and Lakshman away to the underworld and kill them. I shall handle the rest of the raggedy army," said Ravana.

Ahiravan thought for some time. He did not want to enter a situation that had nothing to do with him. But on the other hand he knew who these two brothers were. They were the declared enemy of every demon in all the three worlds. During their forest exile, they had killed many of Ahiravan's friends, and demon well-wishers. It would be satisfying to capture them and have them at his mercy.

"All right. I shall do as you wish." he said to Ravana. "I shall capture them in the night, and when you see the light of dawn, you shall know they are in my power." With this, he bowed and went away.

Ravana felt some relief at the thought that his enemies would shortly be captured by such a mighty demon.

That night, when all was quiet and still, and when the tired warriors of Rama's army slept under the protection of Hanuman, Ahiravan arrived to capture Rama and Lakshman. He saw that Hanuman had lengthened his tail to form an immense circle around the sleeping army. No one could enter the army tents without Hanuman sensing it. Ahiravan thought a while, and remembered that Vibhishan, the brother of Ravana was now an able and trusted fighter on behalf of Rama. He decided to impersonate Vihhishan, to escape detection.

Hanuman was astonished when he saw the figure of Vibhishan walking towards the tent where Rama and Lakshman lay sleeping.

"What is it, brother Vibhishan?" he questioned. "Why are you out in the dead of night?"

"I had gone to say my prayers by the sea, and must have fallen asleep," replied the cunning Ahiravan continuing to walk away from Hanuman. Ever vigilant Hanuman was surprised, and suspicious too.

But he did not want to seem impolite to someone whose help had been of such value to Rama. Thinking this was Vibhishan, he let the intruder pass.

Ahiravan entered the tent where Rama lay sleeping in the midst of his soldiers. Muttering a powerful mantra to make everyone who was sleeping nearby unconscious for a few moments, he picked up Rama and Lakshman and vanished skywards with them. As he swooped down to the entrance of patal lok many miles away, a burst of light in the east heralded the dawn of a new day. Ravana saw it and felt happy.

He had no doubt that Ahiravan would have captured Rama and Lakshman.

Meanwhile, there was terrible confusion in the camp of Rama's army when Sugreev noticed that both Rama and Lakshman were missing. Discussion among them made them realise that the person claiming to be Vibhishan when questioned by Hanuman must have kidnapped the brothers.

"I never left Rama's tent the entire night," said Vibhishan. "But I think I can guess who must have impersonated me. It is something impossible for the demons surrounding Ravana to do. This episode reveals the evil genius of Ahiravan, the demon king of the underworld."

Hanuman s powerful brain was working fast. "No matter who has taken Rama and Lakshman, or where," he declared, "I shall soon catch up with them. Just tell me more about this Ahiravan. Where is the entrance to the underworld? And what do you know about the underworld kingdom?"

Vibhishan quickly told him all that he remembered about the demon world of patal lok Then he, Jambavant, Sugreev, Angad, and the other warriors promised to keep the battle alive without revealing to Ravana that Rama, Lakshman, and Hanuman were all away.

There was a terrible light in Hanuman s eyes, now burning brown fire. "Should that ten headed demon come here himself, I want each person to fight him till death, understand? I shall do my best to bring Rama and Lakshman back as soon as I can."

He was off like a shooting star, with the words 'Jai Sri Ram' on his lips.

Hanuman reached the entrance to Ahiravan's underworld kingdom and was amazed to see a huge monkey with a strong resemblance to himself, guarding the city gates. He made himself as small as a fly, and was trying to slip past this guard, but the monkey's keen eyes saw him, and he was challenged immediately.

"Hey you! Do not try to slip past me in this manner. Don't you know I am the son of the mighty Hanuman, and none dare cheat me!" said the guard.

Hanuman was so shocked by these words that he changed into his normal size without realising it. "What?!" he shouted. "That is a lie! You cannot be the son of Hanuman, since he took a vow never to get married when he was a mere child! Besides," he added, "I am Hanuman, and I have no children. How can you call yourself my son?"

The monkey guard immediately bowed before Hanuman. "My name is Makaradhwaj, father, and the story of my birth is a strange one. When you had finished burning Lanka, you stopped by the sea to rest a few moments, and drops of your sweat fell into the ocean. One of these was swallowed by my mother, who was a large fish!"

Hanuman's eyes were turning round at this strange tale.

"One day my mother was caught in Ahiravan's fishing nets, and when she was taken to the kitchens to be served at dinner, the servants were stunned to find me inside!" It seemed as if Makaradhwaj was enjoying the effect of his story on Hanuman, who was truly taken aback. "I was accepted like a son by Ahiravan, and I will therefore protect this kingdom, even if I have to fight you, my own father," said Makaradhwaj in a voice suddenly full of menace.

Hanuman snapped out of the trance into which Makaradhwaj's story had thrown him. He began wrestling with the giant monkey, and soon succeeded in tying him with his own tail to the gates of the city.

"I must see to the safety of my Lord, Sri Rama," he told Makaradhwaj with a hint of apology. "We will meet again!"

Hanuman entered Ahiravan's palace and found the stage set for a huge sacrifice. A large idol of the goddess Chamunda had before it all the offerings for a special puja, Trays of sweets, fresh fruits, and the most fragrant flowers were arranged for the puja that Ahiravan was to perform. Hanuman hid behind the idol of the Devi, and immediately, She disappeared into the ground. In Her place, Hanuman now stood,with his tongue outstretched, and his arms spread out. This was Devi's way of helping Hanuman in his task of protecting Rama.

The choice offerings of food were all put before Hanuman, in his guise as Devi, and he had every one of them. Puris, halwa, laddoos, all disappeared into his mouth in a steady stream! This adventure was proving to be tastier than Hanuman had thought. With so much food disappearing, Ahiravan's courtiers began to worry if there would be enough.

Ahiravan, wearing blood-red clothes, and drunk with self-importance, prepared for the next stage of his evil worship. He gathered blood-red flowers for his puja, and asked at the appropriate moment for the sacrificial prisoners to be brought in. Rama and Lakshman were brought with their hands and feet bound. They stood together while they were anointed with special oils and incense, in preparation for being offered to Devi.

The moment had an awful sense of finality. Ahiravan could not hide his air of gloating on this frightening occasion. Lakshman was completely puzzled by his brother's behavior. Why had Rama allowed things to reach such a stage? Why did he not destroy the demon, or instruct Lakshman to do it instead? Such a meek acceptance of approaching death seemed completely unnatural to Lakshman.

Lakshman turned towards Rama, looking puzzled. In a voice free of fear or anger, Rama said, "We must now remember our saviour, since death seems so close." Lakshman continued to look at Rama, more puzzled than ever. As if to explain what he meant, Rama went on, "When ordinary humans are close to death, it is customary for them to remember Me. As for Myself, when I find myself in a situation like this, I can think only of him who has always saved me in such times."

At Lakshman's still not understanding him, Rama said, "Yes, Lakshman, I can think only of my beloved Hanuman, my brave Mahabalaya. In fact, I am thinking so deeply of him that even the Devi before us seems to me to resemble him!"

These words from his Lord were all that Hanuman was waiting for. With a great roar, and one giant leap, he landed in the middle of the sacrificial ingredients. In a trice, he had snatched up Ahiravan's sword, and with this he slashed out at his demon-soldiers. As a final assault, he killed Ahiravan, flinging him into the sacrificial fire. Then, carrying Rama and Lakshman on his shoulders, just like he had done on the first occasion of their meeting, he prepared to speed his way back to the battlefield.

At the gate of Ahiravan's city he hesitated before Makaradhwaj, bound by his own tail. Rama, learning who Makaradhwaj was, asked Hanuman to appoint him king of the underworld kingdom in place of Ahiravan.

So Hanuman's new-found son was placed on the throne by Lakshman. The satisfied trio of Rama, Lakshman and Hanuman returned to the battle with Lanka, where their followers awaited them.

The sight of them sent a wave of happiness through the brave monkey-bear army,

"Long live Sri Rama! Long live Lakshman! Long live Hanuman!" they shouted. Ravana heard their joyous shouts and a feeling of dread closed around him.

Prabhu ki kripa bhayau sab kaaju,
janm hamaar suphal bha aaju.

It is due to the grace of Rama that all has been
achieved, and my very birth has found meaning...

A Glimpse Of
The Hanuman Heart

Rama returned to Ayodhya after defeating Ravana. When he occupied the throne as their king, it was the happiest moment in the lives of all those who lived in Ayodhya.

For years, Rama, Sita and Lakshman had worn rough cloth, wooden sandals, and tied their hair in knots, most unlike the royal personalities they were. Now they were surrounded by loving family and courtiers anxious to serve them. Every imaginable wealth was theirs. They just had to express a wish and it was immediately fulfilled.

But Rama was no ordinary king, whose head may get turned by sudden wealth. He was God in human form, and he stayed exactly the same towards all who met him - loving and supremely generous.

After becoming king, Rama honoured many rishis, saints and scholars with gifts. He called Sugreev, the king of Kishkindha, whose army of monkeys and bears had helped him to conquer Lanka, and garlanded him with a necklace made of precious stones. This shone with such dazzling brilliance that it appeared as if the sun's rays were radiating from it! He gave Sugreev's nephew Angad two amulets studded with sapphires whose blue light made it seem as if night was approaching. He gave Vibhishan, the old and wise Jambavant, and monkey and bear warriors like Dwivid, Maind, Nal and Neel similarly precious gifts,

To his wife, Sita, he presented the most beautiful and priceless 'Muktahar', a necklace of rare and brilliant gems that had been given to him by Vayu, the Wind God. Her beauty seemed magnified a thousand times when she sat in Rama's court adorned with this necklace.

But something was disturbing Sita. She noticed Hanuman, whom she loved like a son, looking longingly at the feet of Rama and herself. It seemed as if he was ever waiting for the moment when he could hug their feet and look up at them with his big brown eyes full of love.

How could Rama have forgotten to give his most loyal and trusted follower anything? Sita wondered at this oversight. She did not know that Rama, who knew Hanuman's heart only too well, had begun a chain of events that would open the eyes and minds of all the gathered Ayodhya personalities.

Sita looked at Rama, and began unclasping the necklace from her neck. She indicated Hanuman with her gaze and Rama correctly understood her intention. "You are free to gift your necklace to whoever you think deserves it, Sita" he said. Sita was waiting for these words.

She called Hanuman to her side, and put the priceless jewel into his hands. "You who have served Rama and me so selflessly, deserve the most precious gift of them all," she whispered to Hanuman.

Hanuman's reaction on getting this necklace was a strange one.

He turned it over and over in his hands, and found that while the gems certainly shone, they did not have the comforting quality of Rama's feet. These feet were what Hanuman loved to touch whenever he got the chance. He smelt the beads, hoping for at least a scent of his beloved Rama or Sita, but the beads seemed scented with some strange perfume. Frustrated, he first scratched his head. Why would Ma Sita give him such an unimpressive present?

Anjaneya decided to explore further. He put one bead experimentally into his mouth, and cracked it with his powerful teeth!

The assembled courtiers, Sugreev's warriors, Vibhishan, and Rama's brothers Bharat, Lakshman and Shatrughna all gave a collective gasp. What strange behaviour was this? In a horrified daze, they saw Hanuman peer inside the broken gem. He shook his head in disappointment, and went on to bite another one. Cracked pieces of precious stones began to lie all around Hanuman. Although no one dared scold him, people began whispering among themselves. "After all, Hanuman is only a monkey. What will a monkey know about the value of such rare gems?" said some of them to each other.

Hanuman put another precious bead into his mouth, preparing to crack it, and Vibhishan was moved to ask, "What are you doing? Why are you destroying such a beautiful jewel?"

"Dear Vibhishan, I thought Ma Sita was giving me this necklace because it contained the image of Rama and Sita. But I keep looking into each bead, and have yet to find them. How can it be called a beautiful jewel? Any necklace that does not contain Rama and Sita's beloved image is worthless, just a heap of stones!" said Hanuman.

Vibhishan was taken aback by this explanation. But he could not tolerate the destruction of such a precious necklace. In an exasperated voice, he asked, "How do you expect these gems to contain your Rama and Sita? Why, next you will be saying that they reside in your huge and hairy body!"

Hanuman paused in his task of examining the necklace. Looking directly at Vibhishan, he said with great confidence, "Of course, my Lord and Sita live forever in my heart. Why, I should consider myself worthless indeed, if I forgot them for an instant!"

So saying, he put both hands to his chest. In a single movement, using all his strength, Hanuman tore apart his flesh and revealed his heart, beating inside his chest. To the utter amazement of everyone present, the figures of Rama and Sita were clearly seen, seated above his heart. It seemed to those who were watching, as if the Rama and Sita they saw sitting on the throne had a mirror image – inside Hanuman! Not only this, a sweet sound of 'Rama, Rama' accompanied each breath that Hanuman took.

What was this love that had reached deep inside every atom that made up Hanuman?

No wonder he was often called 'Rambhakt' or Rama's devotee, or 'Rameshtaya', one who was loved by Rama.

The crowd assembled in Rama's court was spellbound. Rama himself stepped down from his throne and gathered up his friend in his familiar embrace. At his touch, Hanuman's chest became whole again, and his face was covered with delight - a delight that even the priceless 'Muktahar' had failed to produce!

That night everyone in Ayodhya who had witnessed this scene was forced to think before they went to sleep, 'What is more precious, wealth or the love of God?' And remembering Hanuman every single one of them knew the right answer.

Ajar amar gunanidhi sut hohu, karahu bahut raghunayak chhohu.

May you be blessed with immortality and serve your Lord Raghunath in many many ways!

A Yawn Too Far

Hanuman's life in Ayodhya made him more content than he had ever been. What more could he ask for? His Lord Rama was the king, and he was able to be near him and Sita, who was like a mother to him.

Hanuman was very happy, and his devotion to Rama was a wonderful example to others. But sometimes this devotion landed him in strange situations too.

One Tuesday morning, Hanuman went up to Sita, and said, "Ma, give me some breakfast. I'm really hungry."

"Dear Hanuman, just give me a minute to bathe and get ready, then I shall be happy to serve you myself," said Sita. Hanuman always seemed like an innocent child to Sita. She loved him for his pure heart, his lack of ill-will towards anybody.

Sita finished her bath. As she did everyday, she picked up a pot of red 'sindoor' (kumkum powder), to put a dot on her forehead, and another dot of it in the parting of her hair. Hanuman was observing this, and suddenly asked, "Why do you do that, Ma?" Sita was astonished by this simple question. Then she laughed and explained, "I put this sindoor on, because it adds years to Rama's life if do," she said. Sindoor is a symbol of married life in India, and women wear it daily. Sita was expressing the popular belief about sindoor.

But she had reckoned without Hanuman's extraordinary devotion.

He was thinking, "If Ma puts a small dot of this red powder and it adds years to my Lord's life, then how many years will be added if I were to cover myself with it!" He had no sooner thought this, than he rushed to get a sufficient amount of sindoor. He sat himself down in a corner, and rubbed his whole body with the red powder, breakfast completely forgotten.

In this completely reddened state, he arrived in the court before Rama. All the people present began to laugh, and Lord Rama himself had a smile, as he asked, "What is the story behind this new look of yours, dear Hanuman?"

Hanuman told him of how Sita had told him that sindoor added years to Rama's life. Since his main desire was to do this, he had thought a mere dot was not enough. That's why he had covered himself with it! Rama was amused by his friend's simple logic of making the quantity of sindoor equal to years of life. He was also extremely touched by

Hanuman's desire for his own long life.

He gave his friend the hug that Hanuman always sought, then announced, "Hanuman is most devoted to me. There is no other like him. In honour of this moment, I declare that whosoever covers Hanuman with sindoor on Tuesdays shall make me extremely happy and earnmy blessings."

This is why the tradition of covering Hanuman idolswith jasmine oil and a heavy orange coloured sindoor became so prevalent in north India. This sindoor coating is called chola or robe and people praying at Hanuman temples are given a dot of this on their foreheads. As far as prayers go, praying to Hanuman is like praying to Rama and vice versa. When Hanuman is praised it pleases his Lord immensely!

But Hanuman's worship of Rama was not without problems. He ran into difficulties with Rama's family on one memorable occasion in Ayodhya.

One evening, Ram's three brothers, Bharat, Lakshman and Shatrughna approached thir sister in law with some hesitation.

"Respected Sita, we need your help," said Bharat.

"What help can I give you?" asked Sita. "It will be a pleasure for me to bring you happiness in any small way I can," she added.

"We are depressed because there does not seem to be any way we can serve our beloved brother Rama," said Bharat who had spent many years being separated from Rama.

"Everything we would like to do for Bhaiyya is already anticipated and performed by Hanuman," explained Lakshman. "I never get the opportunity to even fan him when he sleeps," said Shatrughna in an aggrieved voice.

Sita was surprised to find herself in agreement with her three brothers in law. "You know, I would not have said it myself," she said, thoughtfully. "But now that you have pointed it out, it is true that I myself never get to do any significant service for my own husband. Whatever he needs done is done immediately by Hanuman."

"We have thought of a way out of this, if you will help us to see it through," said Bharat. "What is it?" asked Sita.

The brothers produced a long scroll on which all the duties to be performed for Rama had been written in the form of a table. These included minor tasks like setting his crown on his head, slipping his feet into his regal footwear, and major duties like seeing to his horses, and cooking his meals. Seasonal and ceremonial tasks to serve him before important functions, or while receiving other royal guests, were also included in the table. Each task had a name next to it, showing who was the person to perform it. Not a single task said 'Hanuman'.

"We request you to get Bhaiya to sign on this document," said Bharat. "And let an official seal of the court be put on it to make it complete," said Shatrughna. Sita promised to do what she could.

That night, she produced the scroll and said to Rama, "Please sign on this important document for me."

"What is it?" asked Rama. "Oh, just a list of the duties to be performed for you. We thought we will give each job to somebody, so that everyone gets a chance to serve you," said Sita.

Rama read the entire list very carefully. He noticed there was no work at all assigned to Hanuman, and scented a conspiracy. However, he merely smiled and said, "Very well," and put his signature on the scroll. "And tomorrow, we want this to have the official court seal put on it," added Sita. "It shall be done," said Rama, in his usual calm and unworried manner.

The table of duties had no sooner come into effect than Hanuman was stopped by Shatrughna as he attempted to fan his Lord. "This is my task, dear Bajrang Bali," said Shatrughna. "Please refer to the new official table, listing out everyone's duties."

Hanuman was baffled, but immediately asked to see the official-looking scroll. "But this table does not give me any work to do for my master, my dearest Sri Rama!" cried out Hanuman.

"Never mind. If there is anything else you can think of doing for Bhaiya, you are welcome to add it to the list," said Lakshman, whose conscience had been pricking him about giving Hanuman such a bad deal.

Hanuman scanned the list, which was very detailed indeed, and his lightning-fast brain immediately found a gap. "Who will snap their fingers to keep away mosquitos and insects from entering Sir Rama's mouth when he yawns?" he asked.

"You do that, dear Hanuman," said Lakshman kindly.

"I want it made into an official proclamation too, with my Lord's signature and the court seal," said Hanuman, waving the scroll listing everyone's tasks.

And this was duly done.

Now Rama's family found themselves in a worse position than they had been before. On the first day of his new, officially appointed duty, Hanuman did not leave Rama's side for a second. After all, who could tell when Sri Rama would yawn? It was impossible to foresee!

It became important for Hanuman to stay constantly by his side, with his fingers poised in a 'snap' position! That day, Hanuman ate his meals hurriedly, absent-mindedly, with his left hand, while his right hand remained ever ready to meet Sri Rama's yawn.

By evening, his constant nearness to Rama had got on everyone's nerves. When he made as if to accompany Rama into the sleeping chamber that his Lord shared with Sita, she would have none of it.

"You can resume your duties in the morning," she told him. "Now shoo!"

Poor Hanuman! He retired to the roof of Rama and Sita's bedchamber, and sat there looking up at the stars. A great worry was gnawing at him. Who knew when Sri Rama would yawn? And if he, Hanuman were not there to perform his signal service, what a shame it would be! Thinking thus, Hanuman began saying the name of Rama constantly, snapping his fingers along with his chant.

Sri Rama was no ordinary king of Ayodhya. He was God himself, and when any true devotee calls on God, he is bound to reply. Besides, Hanuman had not eaten properly, and he was consumed by only one thought - to serve his Lord in the event of his yawning. As Hanuman chanted and snapped his fingers, below him Rama began to yawn, as if in reply.

First one, then two, then three, he kept on yawning with increasing speed till he could yawn no more, and his jaw stayed open, completely tired from yawning.

Sita screamed and called her mother-in-law. Rama's brothers assembled, physicians were called, and medicines given that did not produce any results. The constant keeping open of his mouth was now causing Rama's eyes to water too, and it seemed as if he was crying, and could not speak to anybody. Every assembled person was in agony.

They rushed to call Sage Vashisht, Rama's guru. When Vashisht entered and saw what had happened, he was amazed that Hanuman was absent. "Where is Ramdoot?" he asked.

In a tone of apology, Sita told him what had happened. "We have been unjust to dear Hanuman," she admitted to the Sage. "And just before we went to sleep, I shooed him away from being near his Lord!"

A search was immediately begun for Hanuman, and Sage Vashisht discovered him on the roof, chanting and snapping his fingers. He shook Hanuman's shoulders, breaking the trance he had fallen into.

Hanuman leapt up, and then bent down to touch the sage's feet. At that moment, Rama's mouth closed in sheer relief, and he said, with a touch of humour, "Please assign some other work to that most devoted friend of mine."

He need not have worried. That day, the inseparable bond between Rama and Hanuman was so clearly seen that no one questioned Hanuman's right to serve his Lord in any Way he chose, ever again.

The Name Holds Good Forever

Sage Narada is an interesting and intriguing figure from many stories involving gods and goddesses. A great devotee of Vishnu, the Sage is often described wandering about, playing the Veena and chanting 'Narayan, Narayan...'. So many stories are told about him, that it is difficult to know when he actually roamed this earth. However, one thing is sure - he loved to play mischief, and often created some really difficult situations by putting humans and gods to the test.

One such occasion brought Rama and Hanuman on the brink of a fight with each other. Was such a thing possible, ever? Read on to find out how this happened.

One day, the king of Kashi was headed for Ayodhya in a small procession with his most loyal courtiers. This group was going to receive Sri Rama's blessings. While going through a wooded valley, they met Sage Narada, and the king stopped to greet him and pay his respects, As he bowed before Narada, the sage asked the king where he was going. "I am going to Ayodhya, to bow before Sri Rama and get his blessings," said the king. "All of us have been waiting to meet him ever since he became king."

"Hmm..." said Narada, thoughtfully. "Your intention is noble indeed. But there is something you must do, for your visit to be even more rewarding," he continued.

"What is it, respected sage? I am ready to do whatever you advise," said the king.

"Then remember, in the court of Ayodhya, bow low before Sri Rama, but ignore the Sage Vashisht, who is his guru, and sits near him, on a separate throne," said Narada.

The king was startled. "Why, respected sage? Why must I show such poor manners?" he was moved to ask.

"That you shall find out yourself," said Narada mysteriously, and moved on, leaving the king and his companions to proceed to Ayodhya.

Meanwhile, in Ayodhya, Hanuman approached Rama and said, "My Lord, all is well here, and how else can it be, when you are king? Permit me to go and visit my mother for a few days. She is always happy to see me, and I feel blessed to be with her."

"Dear friend, go and make your mother happy!" said Rama. "And do not forget to give her the love and goodwill of all of Ayodhya, especially its' king."

Hanuman left to see his mother, and the king of Kashi arrived to meet and be blessed by Rama. Mindful of what Narada had told him to do, the king ignored Rama's guru, Sage Vashisht.

The elderly sage said nothing at that moment. But no sooner had the king of Kashi retired to the guest chamber, than he complained to Sri Rama, "You are the soul of ethics, and the guardian of all that is good, just and proper," said Sage Vashisht to Sri Rama. "It is not fair that any wrong, even a breach of etiquette, should be committed under your very nose!"

"When was such an act committed, and by whom?" asked Rama, knowing that his guru would not seek to point out any problem to him without reason.

"I was sitting right next to you, in full view of the court, but that insolent king of Kashi only bowed and greeted you," said Sage Vashisht. "He pretended not to see me at all."

Rama's face became grave and his eyes looked briefly troubled.

"Was our guest indeed so daring, as to ignore my guru in my presence? Well, he shall not have long to gloat over this fact. He may be an honoured guest, but this does not give him the right to go against our ideals. I vow to free him from his life by this evening, with these three arrows!" So saying, Rama took out three powerful arrows from his quiver, and kept these at the feet of his guru.

There was complete shock in the court. The news spread like wildfire, and the king of Kashi heard it in a few moments in his guest chamber. He went pale, and immediately felt thirsty. Rama was the most illustrious king from the 'Raghukul' dynasty. The motto for Raghukul went somewhat like this, 'Rather lose our life, than give up our word.' If Rama had indeed promised to finish off the king of Kashi, his death was certain, and there was no getting around it.

The king cast off his ceremonial welcome clothes and slipped into ordinary ones. He left quietly and reached the forest where he had met Sage Narada. The sage sat peacefully, his Veena beside him on the green forest floor. The king of Kashi addressed him with great agitation. "What sort of a problem did you land me in? I did not greet his guru, and now Rama has vowed to kill me by this evening! He has even earmarked the arrows meant for me!" said the king, shouting in his anxiety.

Sage Narada smiled a mysterious smile. "Why consider yourself lost when you have not prayed to him whom even Rama regards as his saviour? Your best chance to stay alive is to go to Anjana, the old mother of Hanuman, and ask her to help you in saving your life. Do not stay content till she has thrice promised to do all she can."

The king of Kashi thought it was very strange to be shunted about in this game that Narada seemed to be playing. But there was no time to argue about that. He rushed with all speed to Anjana's home, and found her happily cooking for Hanuman. Arrived home after a long time, Hanuman had just stepped out into the forest to greet some of his childhood friends.

The king did not waste much time on greetings.

He fell sobbing at Anjana's feet, and she was moved to ask, "What is it son? How can I help you? What can I do?"

"O Ma!" sobbed the king. "A very powerful person has vowed to kill me by this evening. Please give me help and shelter me!" Anjana was touched by the king's plight. "I will do what I can," she promised.

But the king was not content till she had made this promise thrice.

Then he dried his tears, and got up. "But tell me, who is this powerful person whom you fear greatly?" asked Anjana."'Sri Rama, the king of Ayodhya," was the answer she got. Then the king left speedily for Ayodhya, where he could not be seen to stay absent for too long.

Hanuman found his mother in deep thought, staring into the flames of the cooking fire when he returned home. He immediately asked her what was wrong. When she told him, he looked very serious.

"Please help me to protect this king, dear son," pleaded Anjana. "But my own master, my beloved Sri Rama has vowed to kill him," said Hanuman, very disturbed. He was torn between his duty to his mother, and to Rama. "How can I come between Sri Rama and the keeping of his promise?"

"I am sure you will think of something," said Anjana, looking hopefully at her son. And she was right.

In a little while, Hanuman asked her if he could return to Ayodhya, so that he could deal with the crisis brewing there. She agreed, and he was soon by the side of Rama, where, in a completely uncharacteristic manner, he asked his Lord for a favour.

"Hanuman! How delightful to see you again! But I thought you would be spending a few days by your mother's side," said Rama greeting his friend.

"I did go, dear Lord, but have returned to ask of you an important boon," said Hanuman. "What is it?" asked Rama with some surprise. "I am very happy you have asked for anything at all. Usually you never ask anything for yourself, only carry messages and requests from a hundred others," said Rama. Everyone, from Vibhishan to Angad to

Sugreev, sent their pleas to Rama through Hanuman, so that these carried more weight with Rama.

"This time, my request is for myself alone," said Hanuman, with great seriousness. "I want the power and the exclusive right to guard your name. I will guard it with my life, and give protection to any creature who is chanting it," said Hanuman.

"So be it," said Rama, equally seriously. "You have the right to guard my name, and protect all who are praying to me."

Hanuman folded his hands in surrender, bowed, and withdrew.

He took the king of Kashi aside and said, "It will soon be evening. Your only chance to save your life is to come now to the river Sarayu, and pray standing in her holy waters. Do exactly as I say."

The grateful king immediately accompanied Hanuman to the river bank where citizens of Ayodhya were gathering for their evening prayers. Hanuman asked the king to stand waist deep in the sacred Sarayu, and say 'Rama, Rama, Rama...' without stopping. The king folded his hands, closed his eyes, and began to chant.

In the palace, Rama observed the approach of evening, and picked up the first arrow with which he was to shoot the king. He stretched his bow, and released the arrow.

In ancient times, it was possible to shoot arrows that would search for the person for whom they were meant. This was done by using powerful mantras, and it made the arrows intelligent weapons that only destroyed the person they had been sent to destroy. Rama's arrow left his bow and reached the spot where the king of Kashi stood chanting the name of Rama. It whizzed around his ears, baffled as to how to destroy a person who was taking its' masters name without pause. After a few minutes, it gave up and returned to the palace to lie in a disconsolate heap at Rama's feet, ashamed not to have been able to fulfil its mission.

At the Sarayu ghats, Hanuman instructed the king of Kashi further. "Add Ma Sita's name to your chant. Do not let here be any pause in your prayer."

The king of Kashi now began saying 'Sitaram, Sitaram, Sitaram…' He was anxious to save his life and this gave his chant an urgency that increased its power.

Hanuman paced up and down on the river bank, ready to defend his Lord's name, and protect the king's life with his own. He kept his mace, or 'gada' ready for attack, poised on one shoulder.

The second arrow arrived, whizzed about in puzzlement, and left like the first one, to lie shame-faced at Rama's feet. Besides this, a messenger came running and said breathlessly to Rama, "O King! Your faithful servant Hanuman is pacing up and down near the Sarayu river, armed with his formidable 'gada'. As long as he is there to guard the king of Kashi, none can disturb him. The king is chanting without pause, 'Sitaram, Sitaram…'." The messenger's voice trailed away at the sight of Rama's face.

Rama's brow was black as thunder. His normally peaceful and loving expression looked most forbidding. He said between clenched teeth, "So this is why he sought that boon! To prevent me from carrying out my vow! Well Ramdoot, you shall not remain Ram's messenger much longer, if you persist with this deceit."

With these words, Rama picked up his last remaining arrow, and prepared to walk with an awful tread to the bank of the river Saryu.

At the river bank, things were not placid or peaceful. Everyone present was most anxious about what looked like a fight brewing between Rama and Hanuman, his most faithful devotee. How could one harm the other? Such a thing was hard to imagine.

Both Sage Vashisht, and his frequent rival Sage Vishwamitra were present on the occasion. Vishwamitra decided to intervene in what he thought would be a calamity. He went up to Hanuman. Ramdoot was now using his power of 'prana' or life-breath to breathe more life into the poor king of Kashi, who was growing hoarse and breathless from keeping up his chant. Now he was saying, 'Sitaram Hanuman, Sitaram Hanuman...' under Hanuman's instructions.

Vishwamitra said to Hanuman, "Let this foolish king get killed at Rama's hands, Hanuman. Dying at the hands of God is great fortune indeed. But losing the friendship of God would be the worst thing that could ever happen in this world or the next!"

Hanuman turned to Vishwamitra and his eyes were bright brown, even twinkling with a secret amusement. He said, "As you have rightly pointed out, respected sage, dying at God's hands is a blessing indeed. What could be a more fitting way for me to leave this body than to be freed by Rama, while doing the wonderful duty of guarding his name, and protecting one who chants it?"

Vishwamitra stared at Hanuman, and realized it would be a waste of time to try and convince such a completely unconcerned person about saving his own life. He decided to try telling the king of Kashi instead.

"O king most foolish," he hissed. "there you see before you that Sage Vashisht. Even if he is undeserving of such an honour, fall at his feet now, before Rama arrives here. Otherwise you are coming between Rama and Hanuman. Do you understand?"

The king needed no more prodding. In a wet, repentant heap, he fell before Sage Vashisht. The sage kept a hand on the king's head and said, with tears in his eyes, 'I forgive youl'

Rama arrived to see this and was immediately told by his guru. "I have forgiven this man for the insult he handed out to me in your court. You need not strive any further to punish him for my sake."

With the last arrow still in his hand, Rama now looked across at Hanuman. The unrepentant monkey was smiling! And in response to that, Rama smiled too - a sight of such brilliance, that all the Ayodhya citizens who were gathered on the spot gasped 'Aah!' in sheer delight.

As for Hanuman and his Lord, they still looked at each other. It was as if the crowds had just been wiped away for both of them.

Rama stood humbled by the sheer love of his truest devotee. Never could his name be in any danger in the world, as long as Hanuman was around to protect it. In his hand, Rama crushed the last arrow to pieces. Strength wilted before the sweet stubbornness of a pure heart.

Miles away, in the deep green forest, the ageless Sage Narada, sensing what had happened, slowly nodded his head, and smiled too.

Ab mohi bha bharos, Hanumanta,
binu Hari kripa milahi nahin santa.

Now I am convinced, O Hanuman,
good people cannot come into
our lives without the grace of God.

An Unblemished Horoscope

Years after the events of Rama's defeat of Ravana, an elderly Hanuman sat by the sea near the famous bridge of floating rocks or 'Rama-Sethu' that the monkey army had built. It was by stepping on these stones that Rama had been able to cross the ocean to Lanka where he fought and defeated Ravana who had abducted his wife, Sita.

This place by the sea was one of Hanuman's spots for meditating on Rama.

After Rama had been the king of Ayodhya for many years, it was time for him and all who had loved him in his lifetime to ascend to heaven. At that time, Rama had placed his hands on Hanuman's shoulders. Looking deeply into his brown eyes, he had asked him, "Will you accompany me to heaven, or will you stay as the guardian of my name, here on earth? Knowing you are here to protect good people will be a great relief to me. You are like a brother to me, and I want you by my side. But your courage and strength, your kindness and compassion for the weak, and the meek, make me feel you are needed here on earth."

How could Hanuman have ignored the appeal in Rama's voice?

He understood that he would best be serving Rama, by forever staying on earth as a mighty force for goodness against evil. He knew that by hearing people sing songs of praise to Rama, he could be happy. He would stay back, he decided, and wherever Rama's name was being said, or sung, he would go to hear it. And whenever he wished, he would sit and meditate on Rama and all they had been through together.

Thus Hanuman is referred to as a 'Chiranjeevi', or one who is forever alive amidst us, He looks for opportunities to enjoy the sound of Rama's 'kirtan', wherever it happens.

So he sat one evening, watching the waves of the ocean lap peacefully against the shore through his half-closed eyes. The scenes of battle, the joy of victory, the look on Rama's face as he thanked Hanuman for bringing the medicine that saved his brother Lakshman's life - his mind was reliving a thousand memories. The setting sun was again lending a golden touch to his body. The truth was, that he was now an old, dignified monkey with grey fur, and his whiskers were turning white, like a snowy frame around his face, His keen memory, and immense strength, were now used only on those occasions when it was strictly necessary.

At this time, Shani, or the planet Saturn, the much-feared son of Surya, was taking a walk along the shore. Shani had spent all his life quite close to his father, and his face was burned black, as was his body. He had red eyes, and hair that stuck out all along his head.

People feared Shani because they believed that if he chose to enter a person's horoscope, that person would face difficulties, and sometimes suffer greatly, till Shani decided to leave.

A person's horoscope is drawn up according to the positions of different planets when he or she is born it is believed that the experiences one goes through rn lrfe can be understood with the help of the horoscope. If Shani plays a major role in someone's horoscope the pandit reading it will often turn pale or murmur 'Oooh' and shake his head.

This was why Shani had an exaggerated opinion of himself. He was very proud of his powers that could cause the mighty to fall, the rich to become paupers, and the patient and hardworking to conquer all obstacles. So Shani strutted on the beach looking for a worthy target for his dreaded curse. His gaze fell on the quiet meditative figure of Hanuman and he walked up to him.

"Hey! Wake up!" he yelled at the monkey who was often called Mahabalaya the Mighty One or Mahaveer the Most Brave.

Hanuman opened his eyes fully and gazed serenely at Shani. "What is it son?" he asked him. "I was not asleep," he added.

"I have heard that you are very strong, that you have carried mountains killed demons and set fire to a whole kingdom for the sake of Rama," barked Shani striking a threatening pose in front of Hanuman.

"What of it?" asked Hanuman still in a quiet voice.

"Let's see what you can do now!" yelled Shani. "Come have a fight with me and let us decide who is the stronger one!" So saying, he grabbed at one of Hanuman's hands and began pulling at him to get up.

Hanuman snatched his hand away. "Go away, son," he said. "Enjoy you walk on this beautiful and historic shore. Why would you want to fight an old monkey like me? Did you know that we are at the exact spot where hundreds of monkey and bear soldiers worked hard to build a bridge across the sea?"

"Don't try to distract me with your tales," thundered Shani. "Why won't you fight? is it because without Rama being present, you are completely powerless? Did your strength desert you the day he went up to heaven? Shani accompanied this taunt with another lunge towards Hanuman's hand.

Before he had finished speaking, Hanuman had jumped up to his full height. He towered above Shani. His hair was grey, but his eyes could still blaze brown fire. He just looked at Shani without a word, and with an untroubled expression on his face, he began coiling his tail around the agitated planet-god.

Longer and longer grew Hanuman's tail, and it coiled around Shani with all his strength behind it. Shani first struggled, then shouted, then began gasping for breath, as the coils closed tighter and tighter around him.

With Shani still wrapped in the tight grip of his tail, Hanuman suddenly said, "This is the hour for me to perform 'parikrama' (walking in a circle around a holy shrine) of the holy bridge." He began walking at some speed to complete a circle of prayer around the Rama-Sethu.

As he walked, Shani was thrown against the ground, against the boulders that made up the bridge, and the spiky plants that grew along the beach. "Ow, ow, wooh!" he yelled. "Stop! Please stop!"

Shani's face and body were completely bruised, but worse was to follow. As Hanuman leapt from one Sethu stone to another, the salty sea water splashed on Shani's bruises and made them burn. 'Yaa-aa- aahl' he began to yell now.

Mahabalaya completed his parikrama and returned to the beach.

He released the exhausted, injured and crestfallen Shani from his tail.

Shani just lay on the beach, unable to even run away.

"Never trouble an old meditative monkey just because you want to show off your strength," said Hanuman. Shani nodded in dumb agreement, He cringed on the ground, with folded hands.

"And listen, one more thing," said Hanuman. Shani looked up at him. "You shall never trouble anyone who loves me deeply, and says the name of my Lord with devotion." He flicked his tail meaningfully.

"Understand?"

'OW-ow-ow!' howled Shani, in memory of his painful journey over the rocks. 'Yes, I understand.' And with this, he took himself off, slowly and painfully, to rub some oil over his aching bruises.

On Saturdays, across temples in India, devotees of Shani still pour oil on him, to give him some relief from the hiding he got from Hanuman!

And on Saturdays, people all over India pray to Hanuman, one of whose names is 'Sankat Mochan', or destroyer of all trouble. The greatest of difficulties described in a person's horoscope can melt away if one prays to Hanuman, is what they believe.

For truly, Hanuman loved his Rama so much that he feared nothing in the universe - there was no place in his heart or mind for fear! By putting Shani in his place, Hanuman proved to us all that a pure and loving heart cannot be moved by superstition. Let a dozen black cats cross his path, or the pandits gasp at his difficult horoscope, When the true devotee of Hanuman remembers Mahabalaya and Rama, he feels no fear at all.

Hanuman Is As Hanuman Does

Out of all the forms of God worshipped in our country, Hanuman provides the best example for us to follow in our lives. If you have read and enjoyed all the stories in this book, you must have become quite familiar with the qualities of this powerful messenger of Sri Rama. A messenger who proved he was a hero time and time again, as he overcame all obstacles to do Rama's work.

Hanuman's most important quality is his love for Sri Rama. This love is expressed as a kindness for all fellow creatures, and a desire to serve, rather than to command. Hanuman sees his Rama in all human beings and living creatures. He does not feel that he should pray to Rama only in a temple while making life very difficult for his neighbours!

Hanuman's humility makes him very difficult to distract from his service of Sri Rama. He does not get his head turned by flattery, or puff himself up with arrogance every time he does something worth admiring. Instead, he gives all credit for everything to his Lord! He also does not spend all his time collecting wealth or thinking only those who are wealthy and powerful are deserving of his love or respect.

Hanuman"s strength is matched only by his courage. He uses this strength to protect and to comfort, not to frighten, or disturb, or destroy. While Hanuman does not hesitate to defend himself against those who attack him, he never takes on the role of an attacker or offender. His strength comes from knowing what he is doing is right. If he had reason to feel that he was committing a wrong, it would make him fear punishment, and he would be as weak as any human.

Hanuman does not get frightened or disturbed by everyday events. His faith in God is so intense that he does not believe in superstitions, ideas like 'bad luck' or good and bad omens. If one has great love for God in one's heart, all times are good times. This is what Hanuman believes.

Hanuman has many simple child and animal qualities to make him extra special and lovable. He believes in hugs and other demonstrations of affection. He likes to dance and leap about. He loves music, and tasty food, especially fruits. He likes all the good things about life, and he makes a monkey sound of contentment to show this, "Grr- grr.."

Above all, Hanuman is very intelligent. He does not get angry, or bitter or worried about anything in life, because he knows that every person, creature and situation is only another string tying us more tightly to God. His mind is vast enough to hold this idea, and not be threatened by it.

Use Hanuman's qualities in your own life, and take your place among the real life heroes and heroines of our time.